"Two babies at once! I'll never have time to go to bed!" she wailed.

Dan began to worry as reality kicked in. It would be unbelievably tough on her. She'd need a lot of support. Now what?

"I can be here with you from now on," he offered, before he could stop himself.

She froze. "What?"

And then she looked up with such an unhappy face that he found himself saying, "I mean it, Helen. I helped get you into this. I think I ought to be here with you, whenever you need me."

Shining eyed, she stared at him with such naked trust that it made his heart turn over.

"You—you mean you're coming back to live here…now?" she breathed.

"Uh-huh."

"Oh, Dan!" she sighed. She seemed to wiggle and stretch with pleasure. Whatever it was, it had a startling effect on his hungry body.

Back by popular demand...

EXPECTING

She's sexy,
successful...
and
PREGNANT!

Relax and enjoy our fabulous series
about couples whose passion results in
pregnancies...sometimes unexpected! Of course,
the birth of a baby is always a joyful event, and we
can guarantee that our characters will become
besotted moms and dads—but what happened in
those nine months before?

Share the surprises, emotions, drama
and suspense as our parents-to-be come
to terms with the prospect of bringing a
new life into the world. All will discover that
the business of making babies brings with it
the most special love of all....

Sara Wood

FOR THE BABIES' SAKES

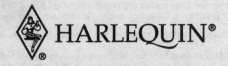

TORONTO • NEW YORK • LONDON
AMSTERDAM • PARIS • SYDNEY • HAMBURG
STOCKHOLM • ATHENS • TOKYO • MILAN • MADRID
PRAGUE • WARSAW • BUDAPEST • AUCKLAND

For Lorna and Karl and their prem babies,
Daniel and Rebecca, who inspired this story and
provided so much personal information. My thanks also
to Heidi for asking them all the right questions!

ISBN 0-373-12280-2

FOR THE BABIES' SAKES

First North American Publication 2002.

Copyright © 2002 by Sara Wood.

This edition published by arrangement with Harlequin Books S.A.

® and TM are trademarks of the publisher. Trademarks indicated with
® are registered in the United States Patent and Trademark Office, the
Canadian Trade Marks Office and in other countries.

Visit us at www.eHarlequin.com

Printed in U.S.A.

CHAPTER ONE

WAS her husband having an affair?

Pale with horror, Helen stood motionless in the hall, so shocked that she didn't notice the mud oozing from her sopping wet suit or the dirty puddle of water that was soaking into the new carpet.

Slowly she closed the front door, her appalled eyes fixed on the very pink, very minimal pair of briefs, resting on the first step of the stairs. She felt too scared to move, in case other intimate items of underwear decorated the rest of the stairs, which disappeared from view in a curving sweep of highly polished oak.

Helen's heart pounded. The briefs were very feminine, and definitely not hers. It was the sort of underwear worn by well-endowed women on the front of saucy magazines. Somehow it had fetched up in her home. But how?

Grey eyes wide, she stared blankly at the ridiculous fringe that decorated the scrap of silky material. Who could own something so uncomfortable and impractical? And what was it doing there in the first place?

Suspicions crowded in on her. Too many things were adding up. She found herself almost incapable of breathing at all. Each gasp of air only increased the choking, bruised sensation in her chest.

Heck, she felt awful. With a small moan, she squeezed her eyes shut, fighting the nausea and weakness of the flu which had plagued her all morning.

Cocking her head on one side, she listened nervously for the tell-tale sounds of an orgy—or female giggles at the very least. Yet with the builders absent for the next two weeks, there was nothing to be heard except the torrential rain, mercilessly battering away at the porch roof. Was this silence good or bad?

Helen shivered and raised a shaking hand to pluck the saturated clothes away from her body. It wasn't the flu that was making her feel so wretched, but a sense of dread. It was sending icy fingers crawling over her skin and chilling her to the marrow.

The facts were beginning to frighten her. One. A sexually active female had dropped those briefs. Helen bit her lip, realising why she'd come to that conclusion. *She* wasn't sexually active. She and Dan were so exhausted from working so hard that they rarely saw one another, let alone found time for making love. And so she wore practical underwear, cotton knickers not men's magazine stuff.

Two. She'd been struggling to put on her wellington boots in the car—a Must Have item with all the rain they'd had that June—when she'd seen that the curtains of the master bedroom had been drawn, even though it was the middle of the day.

She'd been so startled by this that she'd jumped out in disbelief, leaving her umbrella on the passenger seat. The torrential rain had beaten down on her unprotected head while she'd stood looking at the window like an idiot, trying to understand what was going on.

Burglars! she'd thought. And then she'd grinned wryly at her wild imagination because surely burglars wouldn't bother to draw the curtains in one room only while they ransacked the house.

That had led her to fact three. Just one other person had a key to the house. Her husband. Almost in slow motion, she'd turned to look at the barn, where Dan usually parked his car. It was a relief to see it there, rather than a burglars' getaway van with a burly type in a balaclava riding shotgun.

Then she'd realised that Dan must have come home because he'd caught the same flu bug that had laid her low. That was why she had rushed to the house, recklessly scrambling over the huge lumps of soil that had been churned up by the builders' trucks and lorries during the renovations.

Her haste to comfort him had made her careless and she'd fallen flat on her face in the mud, cursing the day they'd moved into the country. Nothing new there. But of course she'd hauled herself up, anxious to provide a bit of TLC, dreaming of cuddles by the fire and nose-blowing in unison.

Huh! He probably didn't have flu at all! Her eyes glowed with resentful anger. Perhaps something else was laying him low! *Someone* else.

She winced, a rush of emotion bringing tears to her eyes. She loved Dan. Adored everything about him. As usual, she was jumping to dramatic conclusions when there was probably an innocent explanation.

But... Female knickers on the stairs. Her husband home. Curtains drawn. It all seemed horribly damning.

A scouring fear washed through her and she felt her legs begin to shake uncontrollably. With a trembling hand she pushed back her hair, smoothing its muddy strands back till it stopped dripping down her face and blurring her vision. She had to investigate.

Hardly aware she was still wearing her muddy boots, she stumbled over to the foot of the stairs and grabbed blindly at the newel post to prevent herself from sinking to the floor in a boneless heap.

Tears dammed up in her throat, choking her. She felt so shocked and weak that she could hardly collect her thoughts to make sense of what was happening.

But she knew there must be a rational explanation. He

wouldn't betray her, not Dan. She racked her brains desperately.

Perhaps he *was* ill. And some time before he'd felt really sick and had come home, he'd bought some sexy underwear to spice up their non-existent sex life, and had accidentally dropped something from his shopping foray as he'd staggered up the stairs to bed.

Her brain stalled, her headache intensifying, and she waited for a moment of dizziness to pass. Illness was so debilitating. She had crawled back from London after nearly fainting on the way to work. The trip had been draining: a long walk, two tubes, an hour's journey on the train and a twenty-minute drive.

Normally she was out all day. Dan would expect her to be furthering her career as the financial executive for the 'Top People's Store' in fashionable Knightsbridge. But she'd come home instead.

And she wished with all her heart that she hadn't because the doubts were building up, terrifying her with the possibility that Dan could be upstairs in their bedroom with another woman.

Her head lifted in despair and, to her horror, she suddenly noticed something else, a few steps further up. It was a nylon stocking in a very fine denier, its twin casually twined around the banister.

'Oh, Dan!' she breathed, tragic-faced, desperately hoping against hope that there was some simple, obvious answer to this. 'Don't be there,' she pleaded. 'I couldn't bear it!'

He was everything to her. She had even agreed to live in this awful house, with its wall-to-wall mud outside and an attic full of crazy squirrels who thundered about all night in clogs. She'd even tried to ignore the spiders who leered at her from every conceivable corner of the house and who waggled their spindly legs at her in a horribly menacing way. Anything, she'd thought, if it made him happy.

And they'd been happy, hadn't they? He'd pledged undying love, had carried her over the threshold of the huge, thatched Deep Dene farmhouse after their marriage two years ago and had proudly pointed out its wonderful potential when all she could see was dereliction and isolation.

But for him she'd put up with the dilapidation, the constant presence of the builders, the temperamental boiler and scowling Aga stove.

City-bred, she had longed for decent pavements, traffic-filled tarmac and frequent inhalations of carbon monoxide. But Dan adored Deep Dene with its ancient beams, inglenook fires and five acres of landscaped gardens, so she had curbed her horror.

They had handed the place over to the workmen and had begun their hectic commuting to London from their future Dream Home in the Sussex Downs. Though it was more of a nightmare to her.

Her stomach churned as she stared blankly into space. Perhaps the commuting was the problem. They hardly saw one another nowadays. It was ages since they'd hugged, and weeks and weeks since they'd made love. She got home late and flung something in the microwave. Dan turned up at all hours, sometimes too shattered to speak.

Her face paled. He was too virile, too intensely masculine to be celibate.

That was when men strayed.

'Dan! Don't do this to me!' she whispered, appalled.

The awful feeling in her stomach became unbearable, though whether that was due to her illness or to fear of what she might find, she didn't know.

Tentatively she lifted a booted foot, vaguely registering that it was thick with clay goo, and put it on the first step of the stairs. As she did so her hair swung forwards in a silky black arc. When she returned it to its proper place behind her ears, she found that perspiration was standing out in beads on her skin. She was sicker than she'd realised.

And then she heard voices. They were faint and distant, drifting down from the master bedroom. But immediately her pathetic theory of Dan's saucy shopping spree was demolished because she clearly identified his firm, low tones and then the lighter purr from an unknown woman.

Her shocked eyes silvered with pain. 'No! *No!*' she denied futilely under her breath.

There was a strange woman in her house. Upstairs. Without knickers. With her *husband*. She swallowed hard. It didn't need a genius to work out the scenario.

Something wrenched inside her, an inner agony that ripped into her heart and sucked away her very breath. She stood there, paralysed with shock, while her head grew dizzy from the manic activity of the horrid little voices, which were whispering in her brain and gleefully suggesting what was going on up there.

She couldn't bear it. She loved him. Trusted him implicitly. It *wasn't* true. There must be some mistake. Had to be.

Perhaps, she thought wildly, there was an alternative to solving the mystery. The coward's way. She could just turn around. Slip out silently. Get into the car and make a lot of noise pretending to arrive. Then she could make believe that this had never happened.

In a stew of indecision she considered this. Pictured herself being fussed over by Dan and the mysterious woman as they fobbed her off with stories of an impromptu business meeting—or maybe pretended the planning of a surprise birthday party...

And then she imagined the questions screaming inside her, for ever silenced by her fear of facing the truth.

No, she couldn't live with herself—or Dan—unless she knew whether he *had* been unfaithful. If he was cheating on her—in her own house, her own *bedroom!*—she must know.

Of course she had no choice but to go up. She was being a wimp. Helen sucked in a huge, rasping breath and eyed the stairs with dread, wishing she could come up with an innocent explanation. Her lower lip trembled. Nothing came to mind. Unless the woman was an interior designer or a fabric expert, who'd, who'd…drawn the curtains to…

Aware that she was floundering, Helen stuffed a fist to her mouth to stop a cry of despair. What about the briefs? The stockings? Who, or why, would anyone drop those? And…now she was peering around the curve of the stairs she could see that there were other…*things* further up, things she hastily averted her gaze from in case they might add up to a confirmation of Dan's infidelity.

Surely he wouldn't! she thought desperately. He loved her. Correction. *Had* loved her. She flushed, the heat flooding through her limp body. How long was it since they'd had time to be loving or even affectionate? Too long. They'd been leading separate lives.

Guilt crawled through every cell she possessed. She'd been too busy, too tired… Her eyes narrowed. It took two to tango. He too had pleaded tiredness! *Tired from what?* a nasty little voice asked and she bit her lip hard.

He'd always crawled in from work exhausted. It was like being married to the Invisible Man. Some days the nearest she got to him in waking hours was ironing his shirts. He wore two a day—sometimes three. After he'd burned two of them with the iron one morning, during his hectic scramble to catch the six-thirty to Victoria, she'd taken over the chore. But now she wondered if she'd merely been smartening him up for his mistress.

A wave of sickness took her by surprise, roaring its way through her. For a moment she remained motionless, waiting till the flush of heat had gone. And then she forced herself to confront Dan even though she dreaded what she'd find.

But her long legs simply refused to take another step. Sinking to her knees, she virtually dragged herself up, avoiding more than a cursory, horrified glance at a pair of discarded shoes which were bright cerise and glove-soft with courtesan heels. Tart's shoes, she thought with unaccustomed viciousness.

A little further on, she encountered a sickly pink bra and suspender belt with a matching silk T-shirt. Beyond, she could see an abandoned navy suit, the skirt and jacket arranged almost artistically on the top step.

Her throat dried. All hope of an innocent explanation lay dead in the water. She dug her teeth into her lip till she felt the pain. Somehow she kept going, each step a mountain to climb as it brought her closer to the terrifying truth. She'd always been determined. And never more so than now.

Somewhere in the background she was aware that Dan and the woman were still talking but she couldn't hear them properly because the blood was roaring so loudly in her ears. They could have been murmuring sweet nothings or discussing curtains to match the pink knickers for all she knew.

Her stomach plummeted like a lift. I love you, Dan! I love you! she screamed silently to herself. Don't do this to me!

And she prayed for this to be a bad dream, a hallucination brought on by flu, that she'd wake up and later she'd tell Dan and they'd laugh and he'd sweep her into

his arms and say that he'd never look at another woman
because he loved her so much and he hadn't minded not
having sex or decent suppers and that he'd neglected her
shamefully...

Oh, God. She'd arrived. The top of the stairs. Still on
her hands and knees, she found to her dismay that she was
weeping and gasping uncontrollably.

And that she was staring straight at a naked pair of
female legs.

CHAPTER TWO

THEY were very shapely, she noted hazily. With scarlet toenails. Helen's world spun around on its axis. She daredn't look any higher. She wasn't ready to be confronted by the full horror of her husband's nude paramour.

'Good grief! Helen!' exclaimed the owner of the legs. 'What *have* you got on your feet?'

Celine's laugh seared through her. Celine, Helen thought dumbly, her gaze fixated on the blood-red toes that seemed to be curling possessively into the landing carpet as if claiming ownership of the house as well as her husband.

This was Dan's PA. His right-hand woman. Angrily she amended that. Include her left hand in that description, too! And both legs, torso, boobs…all of Celine was apparently part of Dan's domain! And the woman wasn't even *embarrassed*!

A sudden fury shot Helen to her feet. Brimming over with outrage, she took in Celine's triumphant and excited air, the carelessly draped blue towel over a stunning body—*her* towel, she thought furiously!—and slowly advanced across the wide landing, knowing she must look like a drowned rat from a sewer but far too mad to care that she shed rainwater and muddy clay all over the cream carpet.

'I'm wearing huge clumping, mucky boots that can do a lot of damage to bare toes!' she choked as Celine backed fastidiously away. And hoarse with anger and misery, she grated, 'Now explain *your* novel outfit, Celine!'

'*Helen!*' came Dan's horrified tones.

Her head jerked back to the open bedroom door where he stood. She closed her eyes tightly and swayed, her energy spent.

All hard masculine jaw and blazing black eyes, he was naked but for the small towel draped around lean hips, steam rising from his fantastic body, his hair wet and appealingly tousled from the shower. A post-sex shower, she thought, with a sharp intake of breath.

It was true then. He'd been unfaithful. Oh, sweet heaven…

'You *swine!*' she yelled furiously as her world crashed about her ears.

'Oh, my God!' Dan groaned.

Wounded beyond belief, she looked into his shadowed eyes and saw embarrassment and sick dismay written clearly for her to see. He was white-lipped, his honeyed skin drawn tautly over his incredible cheekbones. A guilty man if ever there was. Her stomach rolled dizzyingly.

'Dan!' was all she could croak in reproach before her voice shattered into tiny pieces of misery.

A spasm of pain jerked at his features.

'Sweetheart!'

Dark brows drawn together in a frown, he stretched out a conciliatory hand of concern. Helen recoiled with disgust.

'No! Don't touch me!'

He flinched, his glittering eyes narrowed in hurt annoyance.

'You don't understand,' he said sternly. 'It's not what you think—'

'Isn't it? Don't lie to me! Don't take me for a fool!' Helen jerked in near hysteria.

He'd even come up with the classic male response. *It's not what you think.* But it always was.

'I'm not lying!' Grimly he folded his arms over his bare

chest and she realised that, despite his defiant stance, he was having trouble with his breathing. She didn't want to consider why that might be. 'You're jumping to conclusions—'

'You bet I am!' she wailed. 'Look at you! Look at *her*!' Violently she stabbed an accusing finger at the siren in the blue towel. 'Wouldn't you jump to conclusions, too?'

Dan glared ferociously at Celine as if it was all her fault he'd been found out.

'Celine!' he growled. 'I *told* you—'

'I don't believe this! You can't hold her responsible!' Helen burst in, appalled that he was trying to wriggle out of this.

'Why not?' he flashed. 'She is!'

'Oh, for heaven's sake, Dan!' she stormed. 'Don't you have any shame, any sense of responsibility?'

'Celine—'

'No!' she shouted. 'Stop pretending it's not your fault at all. It takes two to get to this stage of nudity! I thought better of you. It seems I was mistaken. I can't believe you can be such a worm as to put the blame on her!' She put icy fingertips to her hot forehead to stem the ache. 'How *could* you do this?' she cried, smoke-dark eyes awash with misery. 'If you cared about me you wouldn't have—'

'*Helen!*' He was frowning at her, his expression shocked.

'What? What is it?' she demanded brokenly.

'You look *terrible*!' he stated with cruel candour.

She winced. 'Thanks a bunch,' she muttered. 'That's all I need, right at this moment.'

Her sullen glance shot to the delectable Celine, who beamed at her and let the towel slip artfully to offer further revelations of her smoothly swelling breasts.

Celine wasn't red-faced and blotchy from weeping. Her

hair hadn't been flattened by the rain, nor had the ends been sluiced by mud into rat's tails.

Helen didn't need Celine's scathing scrutiny to make her aware of the contrast between them. Instead of being sophisticated and irresistible, Helen thought miserably, she was covered in mud and looking terminally ill. A drowned waif in wellies couldn't compete with sex on legs.

Just when she needed to look fabulous, she had to impersonate a rugby scrum-half after extra time.

'Well, you do look rough,' Dan stated, frowning.

'I reckon Cleopatra herself wouldn't look so hot under the circumstances!' she grumped in resentment. Her head flung up in defiance. 'When did the Queen of the Nile ever come home to find *her* husband had ripped the clothes off another woman and flung them any-old-how on the stair carpet?'

'Ripped *what*? Just what are you talking about?' he demanded, a picture of righteous indignation.

'That. There!' she cried bitterly, her trembling finger pointing in the direction of the clothing on the stairs.

He dug up a puzzled expression and wore it convincingly, his long legs covering the ground between them in seconds, impatience in every stride.

'Good grief!' he said slowly, staring at the discarded items as if he hadn't seen them before.

It was a brilliant performance. No wonder he'd successfully hidden his philandering from her, she thought waspishly. Stand back Hollywood. Make way for Dan Shaw and his impersonation of an innocent man wrongly accused.

'Remember now?' she snapped, glaring up at him. 'Or were you in such a haze of lust that you never *noticed* at the time?'

She thought he'd explode with anger. A terrifying rage had taken hold of him, his fury directed at Celine, who put a hand to her mouth in a 'weren't we naughty?' gesture.

'You stupid woman!' he growled savagely.

When Celine shrugged and batted her lashes, Helen feared for the woman's safety. Dan seemed to be visibly swelling with rage, his expression black and thunderous as he sucked in a harsh breath, clearly in preparation for a stream of abuse.

'Don't you take it out on her!' Helen spat, consumed by fury. 'Look to your own failings! You caused this situation! You—'

'*No!*' he yelled, rounding on Helen. 'How many times do I have to say it? I know nothing about this!'

Intimidated by six feet two of muscled fury looming over her, she hastily moved back. He was going to deny the undeniable, she thought in astonishment. Be offended. Make out she was doing him an injustice!

'Really. Were you drugged? Date raped? I can't believe you're denying this!' she muttered.

'It's true!' he protested, but she could see from the widening of his eyes that he was beginning to panic. A nerve was quivering manically in his strong jaw and his nostrils had narrowed with an even sharper intake of breath.

'Please!' Helen jerked, her hand pressing her aching forehead again. 'Save yourself the effort of protesting your innocence. I don't want lies.'

Icy cold with hopeless despair, she lifted pained eyes to his and she almost wept when she saw his answering pity. She did not want pity, either. She wanted rock-solid fidelity.

'I'm *not* lying,' he repeated more quietly. 'And I'll deal with that in a moment. You need sorting out first, Helen. You're wet through and covered in mud—'

'As if I didn't know!' she flung miserably.

His mouth lost all its sensual curves and flattened into a forbidding line as he grunted with irritation.

'Cut the sarcasm. What happened? Did you fall over?' he demanded, in a taking-charge voice.

'Yes, I flaming did!' Huge tears of self-pity welled up, obliterating her vision. 'I s-saw the bedroom curtains were d-drawn,' she stammered, scrubbing crossly at her eyes. 'I saw your car. I-I thought you were ill and I was...worried. Worried!' she flung accusingly. 'Huh! If I'd *known*... But like an idiot I wanted to look after you so I ran and—and slipped in the mud—'

'Oh, my darling—'

All loving concern, he took a step towards her, his arms outstretched to embrace her.

'Don't come near me!' she sobbed, cringing in horror. 'Don't touch me! And don't you darling me!'

He bit his lip and swallowed, the hard-packed muscles of his torso tense with angry apprehension.

'But, sweetheart,' he insisted, 'I swear, you're getting the wrong idea—'

'I'm not, but I wish I was!' she cried desperately. 'OK! Go ahead! Give me the *right* idea. This should be good! I can't *wait* to know why you're both virtually naked and—and—' her voice wobbled '—and why Celine looks so darn pleased with herself!'

'Celine,' Dan said, suddenly icy quiet and remote, 'collect your clothes and...get...dressed...'

Alerted by his halting speech, Helen shot a fierce glance at Celine. The towel around the woman's body had dipped a fraction. Dan was blinking rapidly at the sleepy nipple that had appeared. He seemed stunned, as if his brain had been overcome by lust, and Helen felt her heart sink to her boots.

'Of course,' Celine purred accommodatingly, making sure that her cover-up involved a lot of jiggling around.

Helen gritted her teeth, wanting to slap the woman for being so obvious. 'Don't forget, though,' she fluttered, 'the meeting's in an hour—'

'No!' Dan threaded his fingers through his thick hair, causing small black curls to tumble haphazardly onto his forehead. He was clearly having difficulty getting his mind into gear, Helen thought angrily. 'I... Oh, *hell*. Cancel the meeting,' he said, suddenly decisive. 'Call a taxi and get out of here. Be in my office tonight—'

'Your *office*! I understand,' his PA gurgled sexily.

Dan's eyes blackened with fury as his breath hissed in. 'I doubt it. You'll be picking up your things and never coming back,' he snapped.

Celine's green eyes widened with astonishment and then her face tightened into malicious lines. 'After all we've meant to one another?' she objected. 'Consider what you'll be missing, Dan, shackled to this... boring jumble sale of a woman. We've had such fun. You're one hell of a guy. We're great together, you said so.'

Celine's waggling eyebrows left no doubt in Helen's mind that the woman was referring to Dan's performance in bed. He was spluttering incoherently at Celine's frankness, his fists clenched as if he might hit her because she'd ruined his hopes of lying his way out of this. A wild fury exploded inside Helen.

'You trollop! Get out of my house!' she shrieked. 'Out! Now—or you'll end up needing a wig!'

Celine backed further down the landing and Helen's eyes squeezed shut. Sweet heaven, beside Celine she *was* dull and dreary! Dan's affair had been inevitable. He'd needed more than a stranger who passed in the night, thrust foil dinners at him and ironed his shirts.

That must be why he and Celine had become close. Worse, they had *meant something* to one another. And whatever he'd said, Dan wouldn't sack his PA—she was too valuable an employee. He'd only been making an empty gesture, hoping it would pacify his irate wife and avert a row—because he was an abject coward.

A sob lurched into her throat. She'd thought him to be strong and brave and noble. Mr Reliable-but-sexy-with-it. In a few brief moments his pedestal had come crashing to the ground. Her respect for him had hit the dust and rolled out into the gutter to disappear down the sewers.

She wanted to scream in despair and disappointment. Ever since she could remember, her whole world had been wrapped around Dan. And now she knew there'd never really been anything there.

Dimly she was aware of his low, urgent voice as he spoke to Celine. Helen wouldn't open her eyes. He sounded as if he was close to the woman, perhaps touching her, from the gravelly whispering.

Her marriage was over, she thought dully. Their love in tatters. And suddenly she felt horribly alone and vulnerable.

Hurriedly she clapped a hand to her mouth as her stomach heaved and a wave of heat rushed up her entire body. With a despairing cry, she blundered into the bedroom and headed for the *en suite,* leaving a trail of sticky clay to embed itself firmly in the fibres of the expensive carpet.

Dan had barked something at Celine and then he must have followed Helen into the bathroom because his hands were on her shoulders, ice-cold, heavy, imprisoning, the pressure of his half-naked chest against her back somehow intimate and shocking.

'Darling...' he coaxed, low-voiced and soothing.

Hysterically she shook them off with an impassioned, 'I'm not your darling! Don't pretend you care!'

'Of course I do,' he said sternly. 'I'm worried about you. I think you're ill—'

'I *am* ill! And you're making me feel worse! I came home because I've got flu!' she cried miserably, hanging onto the basin as if her life depended on it. Her stomach churned horribly but she couldn't be sick even though she felt as if she might.

'Then you must get to bed—'

'*Bed!*'

Her eyes met his in the mirror and he flinched from her scything glare.

'What? What did I say?' he demanded thinly.

'Do you intend to change the sheets first?' she hurled in anguish.

He gasped as if she'd lashed him with a whip. She saw his tight stomach muscles contract and recognised the pain that had rocketed through him. He looks ghastly, she thought. And tried not to care.

'I don't *need* to change the sheets!' he grated.

Her eyes widened. Passion had struck somewhere else, then!

'So you didn't make it to the bedroom!' she cried wildly, unable to bear the thought of Dan being so crazy for another woman. 'You couldn't wait, I suppose! Where, then? Tell me so I can avoid that place! Tell me! In the hall? The stairs? I'll burn the carpet,' she threatened. 'Rip up the floorboards. Have them replaced—!'

'Helen! Stop this! You're being irrational—'

'I know!' she cried in distress. He'd made love to Celine. How could she ever get over that? 'And with good reason!' she sobbed. 'You brute! I hate you for doing this to me!'

Unable to control herself, she whirled around and hammered her fists into his naked chest. He let her, taking the blows—presumably because he knew he deserved every one of them. And she was exhausted by her outburst.

'Stop it, Helen. Calm down,' he urged.

'Then tell me what happened! I have a right to know!' she moaned, suddenly going limp in his arms.

'I *will*,' he said gruffly, holding her up. 'Don't upset yourself, *please*. Just trust me—'

'Are you *mad*?' she railed, feeling his strength sustaining her. His wonderfully lithe, powerful body, she thought. Then jealousy struck as she imagined his eyes looking at Celine with desire, his hands touching, arousing... She sucked in a tortured breath, unable to bear it. 'Go away, Dan!' she sobbed. 'I don't want to see you or hear you or think of you ever again!'

'Don't say that!' His grip tightened. His eyes blazed. 'Don't ever say that, Helen! I'm not going anywhere—'

'You'll have to. You can't possibly explain this away.'

Her eyes were dead. She thought she'd never smile again.

'I can. I will. But first you must get into bed before you get pneumonia. You look—'

'I *know* what I look like!' she raged. 'Plug ugly! My hair is a mess and I look worse than a typhus victim. Oh, sidle off to glamorous, voluptuous Celine and leave me to crawl into bed on my own!'

'Poor love. What a hell you're in,' he rasped, stroking her plastered-down hair with a masterly semblance of affection.

And she almost succumbed. She wanted to be loved by him so badly, wanted to be held and cuddled and cosied up so much, that she stood there with her eyes closed, longing, wishing, adoring. Smelling his familiar and much-loved body smell. Feeling his warmth and energy. Hearing that seductively coaxing voice and finding her muscles relaxing in response.

'Come on, darling.'

Her eyes snapped open at the husky coaxing. His fingers were unbuttoning her jacket! Shocked rigid, she knocked his hand away, stricken by the fact that he'd done the same to Celine only a short time ago.

'You—you *animal*! Is that your solution? Is that all you can think about? A quick roll in the hay? Don't you have any conscience, any moral values at all? Just…leave… me…al*one*!' she wailed, beside herself with grief.

'Calm *down*! That wasn't my intention at all. I was trying to help,' he said tautly. 'Or are you intending to get into bed fully dressed?'

'Right now I don't care! Just…don't…touch…me!' she flared.

'Fine. If that's what you want…'

Taking her at her word, he let go and her legs gave way. She slid to the floor, weeping with frustration, racked with misery. A pathetic little heap, she thought. A ludicrous idiot wearing wellies. Oh, how he and Celine would sneer at her later!

'Stupid, stubborn woman!' Dan muttered under his breath.

Angrily he pulled her boots off before she could stop him, flinging them in the bath. She retaliated by curling up in a foetal position, her body shuddering with huge, uncontrollable sobs.

'G-g-go 'way!' she mumbled through her tears, desperate to be alone.

'No.'

Dan ignored her flailing hands and feet and grimly removed her clothes. Once or twice she scored a direct hit on him, judging by his grunts, but he wasn't deterred.

In a hostile silence they wrestled and thrashed around the slippery floor, though her resistance was feeble. When he'd peeled off her stockings and she was down to her bra and pants she gave up the struggle, too weak, too resigned to his determination to humiliate her.

He'd be comparing her body with Celine's. Would be

thinking that women should wear man-trap underwear with lace and fringes and holes and tassels, she thought miserably. Not neat-fitting, passion-killer cotton.

And he'd be secretly glad she'd discovered his affair because that would give him an excuse to leave her and get a decent replacement. Someone svelte and gorgeous who made pets of spiders and loved muddy countryside.

'I feel sick,' she muttered weakly, wondering how the elegant Celine fitted into that description of Dan's perfect woman.

With an exasperated grunt, he tightened his towel around his narrow hips and raised her, wrapping her up in a warm bath sheet. Her shivering body sank gratefully into its soft folds as she held onto the edge of the basin again, wishing she could be sick and get it over and done with.

The nausea subsided and she turned away disconsolately. Dan took hold of her again, towelling her wet hair and then washing her horribly blotchy, tear-stained face. It was dangerously lovely, like being nurtured by her mother when she was a child, after she'd been ill with measles and had been allowed her first bath for a few days.

But her mother hadn't picked her up, or carried her back, to bed and it was this that was almost her undoing. Clutched in the shelter of Dan's strong arms, Helen fought to overcome a fierce urge to snuggle up to the glorious firmness of his naked chest and wrap her arms around his neck. This was her husband. It was the first time for months that they'd been physically close and her hormones were reacting accordingly.

Stone-faced, he undid her bra, his eyes lingering on her breasts. Her hopes rose. Perhaps he did find her attractive, despite everything...

Her spirits plummeted as, without comment, he pulled her sulkily compliant arms into a warm nightdress and tucked the bedclothes up around her neck.

It was then that she saw he was aroused. But was that, she wondered suspiciously, because he and Celine had been disturbed before...before...*it* had happened, and he was still unsatisfied?

Tormented by her thoughts, Helen turned her face away, her eyes tightly shut in a vain attempt to stop the tears from flowing again.

She wouldn't cry. Her head had to be clear, her brain sharp. She had to make plans. Illness was making her act like a victim, but when she felt better she'd stand up for herself and fight for her rights.

The mattress shifted under Dan's weight. His hand came up to brush dark strands of hair from her hot face.

'I'm sorry you feel so rotten. What can I get you, sweetheart?' he asked softly.

'A *divorce!*' she blurted out from the depths of her misery. '*Now!*'

CHAPTER THREE

THERE was a terrible silence. Helen didn't breathe or move, appalled at the finality of what she'd said—and its inevitability. She could feel Dan's shock like a seismic wave and sensed that his muscles were screwed up as tightly as hers.

And then he spoke, in a strangely halting and husky voice as if his heart was breaking, too.

'I'll get you a hot-water bottle and a thermometer. And a hot honey and lemon drink. When you've slept and you feel a little better, we'll talk.'

'Talk now! Before you have a chance to come up with some slippery explanation!' she jerked.

He gazed at her with sad and unnervingly remote eyes.

'Do you trust me so little?' he asked quietly.

Helen felt bitterness scourging her insides. Trust? She would have staked her life on him. He had held her hopes and her love and her future in his hands. And he'd let her down.

She shuddered. It was as if she'd reached the depths of hell and suddenly she wanted to drag him there, too.

'If you came home unexpectedly and found *me* half naked, surrounded by several pairs of boxer shorts and socks, riding boots, assorted spurs, scarlet jackets and a collection of plumed helmets,' she retorted coldly, 'wouldn't you assume I'd jumped into bed with a Brigade of Guards?'

Dan went a sickly colour. His jaw worked as though his teeth were grinding together.

'I'll get that drink.'

He couldn't get away fast enough, she thought, her face forlorn. Not only was she physically ugly to him, but she was showing a vicious, sarcastic side to herself she'd never known had existed. He'd always adored the funny slant she had on life. But now her tongue was turning to acid and burning her as well as him.

Was it any wonder, though, that she felt like lashing out? Miserably she burrowed deep into the bedclothes. She'd surrendered her heart to Dan and he'd rewarded her loyalty with the worst betrayal of all, just two years into their marriage. Of course, she thought glumly, it had been a farce for some time and she hadn't even noticed.

All those late nights when he'd been supposedly expanding his already successful business, working with clients in the evenings and on weekends... He'd been with *that woman*. His exhaustion had been for other reasons than writing software, doing mega-buck deals and travelling around London till all hours of the night.

And, although she adored the career she'd chosen, *she'd* only worked overtime because she'd hated coming home to this vile house, to the emptiness and silence and the half-decorated rooms. Her eyes blazed in fury. All the while, he'd been cavorting with the luscious Celine and wining and dining her—

'Here you are.'

At Dan's voice, she shot up, furious at being deceived for so long. Her hand flew out, knocking the offered mug from his grip. Locking eyes, they both ignored the sticky mixture as it oozed over the duvet. She had questions in her glittering gaze. He seemed to be in deep shock.

'Forget the ministrations. Let's get the explanation over with,' she scowled, secretly appalled by her uncontrollable feelings.

'Better, I think, that it should wait,' Dan said, stilted

and withdrawn as he glared down at her. 'You're clearly in a foul mood—'

'What do you expect?' she spluttered.

'A fair hearing! And I'm not going to get it at the moment, am I?'

Her mouth took on a bitter shape. 'Did you give our marriage a fair chance?'

He blanched. 'Yes. I did.'

'Oh? How long for?' she demanded. 'A week? Or did you manage a month before you started playing the field? How long, Dan? How long has this been going on?'

'It hasn't. I have not been unfaithful,' he said doggedly.

He swallowed and she thought there was the hint of moisture blurring his dark eyes.

Perhaps he was sorry now. There'd be all the problems of splitting up: sharing out the wedding presents and deciding who paid what for the furniture and carpets...

It was a nightmare. No wonder he looked sick.

She heaved in a huge breath. 'You'll forgive me if I find that hard to believe.'

With a face set like concrete, he handed her the hot-water bottle. She contemplated hurling it at the hideous vase his best man had given them, but grudgingly took it. She needed the warmth. Her body was as cold as Siberia.

Dan drew up a chair and sat heavily in it, the towel parting to show an expanse of tightly toned thigh. Incongruously, she wanted to touch the satiny skin.

'Temperature,' he said dully.

So *he* was miserable, she thought, jerking out of her mooning over him. Annoyed with herself for being so easily diverted by his long, powerful legs, she snatched the thermometer from him and stuffed it into her mouth, glowering at him from under her dark brows. After a moment he looked away, unable to hold her gaze. Guilt, she thought, and felt no pleasure in the certainty.

Hauling himself up as if his body were a lead weight, he moved slowly to stand by the window, the beautiful triangle of his back a stiff barrier between them. Incredibly, his dejection upset her. She tried to hate him but her heart kept betraying her efforts.

It was awful seeing someone as confident and unassailable as Dan look so diminished. He'd always given the impression that he could withstand anything that was thrown at him. All his movements had been vigorous and definite, his muscular body brimming with energy.

Now he looked as if the life-blood had been drained from him. Sympathy oozed from her and she felt herself crumple. Feeling weak, she slumped back into the plumped-up pillows, her mouth releasing a soft moan.

He was probably contemplating the future. The house would have to go, for a start. That was why he looked so bleak and depressed. He adored Deep Dene.

Whereas she was dreading the consequences of his adultery for a different reason: because she had loved him with all her heart. She pushed that from her mind, postponing the empty black hole that was her future without Dan.

She gave a little gasping intake of breath, realising that she *still* loved him. Madly and deeply—despite her low opinion of him. You couldn't immediately switch off something that had been all-consuming and magical for years and years. Heck, they'd known one another since their teens and neither of them had ever looked at anyone else. Till now.

Her slender arm lifted and angled to cover her anguished eyes. It would take ages for the hurt to go away— if it ever did. Already it was searing her heart with a cramping agony and her mind seemed to be churning with disjointed thoughts...

The thermometer was slipped from her mouth and she sullenly opened dark and angry eyes to see Dan studying

it, his face still bent over hers, close, touchable, the strong
planes of his face achingly near.

'Well. Let's see.' Low and husky, his voice seeped like
hot lava into her bloodstream, startling her with unwanted
sensuality. Breathing heavily, he stared at her shoulder and
she hastily slid the errant satin shoulder-strap of her
nightie back into place. 'Normal,' he declared in a tone
that was anything but.

Collecting her ragged nerves together, she blinked and
frowned in disbelief.

'Can't be. I feel rotten.'

'See for yourself.'

She did, and was surprised. 'Then I've eaten something
dodgy,' she muttered, unable to take her eyes from the
sultry lines of his mouth.

He straightened, taking away temptation. 'Do want to
sleep, or do you feel up to listening to me properly?' Dan
asked stiffly, the proud carriage of his head telling her that
he was going to brazen this out.

'Sleep? Do you think I could sleep with this on my
mind?' she cried, her body still pulsing with warmth.

'No. Of course not. All right. But on one condition. I
want you to avoid making any sarcastic remarks till I've
finished,' he said in a horribly distant tone.

Suitably chastened, she felt her lip quivering. She
shouldn't behave like a prize bitch. Shock seemed to have
turned her into a different woman, someone who wanted
to lash out and yell and behave like a wounded tigress.
He'd done this to her. Made her no better than an animal.

'I'm sorry. I lost control. I felt...'

'I understand,' he muttered, as if he didn't want her to
spell it out.

Her eyes blinked back treacherous tears. How could he
know how deeply she mourned the man she had loved? How
her very heart was shrivelling because her uncondi-

tional belief in him had been shattered? She felt more than empty. There was nothing good left in her life. Nothing to look forward to.

'I doubt that you do,' she whispered.

He looked down on her with an impassive expression, his tall figure dauntingly rigid.

'It's not surprising you're on edge. You're not well. And you had a shock.'

Helen drew in a shaky breath. They were talking like polite acquaintances. She was apologising for ranting at him, he was making allowances for her. It was bizarre.

Helen nodded, not trusting herself to speak. Helplessly she gazed at his handsome face, which had so often turned her to jelly. Her mouth had kissed those dark and haunted eyes and even now her memory could vividly recall the silk of his thick lashes against the softness of her lips. Her fingers had stroked the fine jaw and she'd marvelled at the strength of the underlying bone. Time after time, her body had lain against his, ecstatic, replete...

And so had Celine's mouth, Celine's fingers, Celine's body.

Anguished, ripped apart by pain, she jerked her head away in a sudden, violent movement.

'What is it?' he enquired urgently, gripping the fragile bones of her bare shoulder. His voice gentled. 'Helen, tell me!' he coaxed. 'Is it a pain? Where?'

Everywhere. She was hurting so badly. And he was trying to get round her with soft words of concern, imagining they could brush this aside and carry on as normal. But she'd lost the love of her life, her hopes for the future, father of her future children...

So many times she'd dreamed of their life together, of another, nicer house they'd have when they'd saved enough, a mews house in Chelsea perhaps; of the dinner parties with good friends; their much-adored children.

Four, she'd thought. To make up for the family Dan had never had, for the bruising childhood and emptiness of his youth. There'd be jolly outings, holidays abroad, a life built on love and happiness, the security of their high-powered jobs.

All for nothing. Because she couldn't ever let him into her heart again.

'Helen!' he muttered in alarm when she screwed up her body in despair. His grip tightened and he shook her slightly. 'Please! What is it?'

'You! Don't you understand? I can't bear to look at you!' she yelled in misery.

Dimly she heard Dan thundering out of the room. To her confusion, she began to sob, because she'd wanted him to be there beside her, stroking, soothing... What a fool she was. It seemed she didn't know what she wanted at all.

Weak and defeated, she slumped against the pillows. Perhaps he was leaving and she'd never see him again. Horrified, she began to wail in earnest, her whole body succumbing to the sense of terrible desolation she felt.

To be alone, without him. Never seeing his face, never hearing his breathing beside her as they lay in bed together, never lovingly and lingeringly smoothing out that dent in his pillow...

Oh, why hadn't she seen the danger signs, noticed that they were neglecting one another, put her foot down and insisted that they had time together?

If only she could put the clock back! Then she'd never know he was really weak and flawed. But...was that so surprising? He'd had such a harsh and unloving upbringing... Maybe, she mused, he'd always covered up his faults, in a desperate attempt to make successive foster parents like him. And so he'd built his life on lies, on a mask that hid his true nature.

She almost felt sorry for him. And consequently was more muddled than ever. But she had to remember that he wasn't the man she'd imagined. She'd married an illusion—and couldn't live with the reality: someone who cheated and lied for his own selfish ends.

'Helen.' His voice was strangled, close to her ear. She put her hands up to shut him out but he hauled her up and roughly dabbed at her streaming eyes. 'Don't cry. Please don't cry,' he said rawly. 'I've brought you some brandy. You must drink it—I insist. You'll be so ill…'

She couldn't be ill. She must be strong and organise her new life. See solicitors. Produce lists of things to do.

The jagged sobs came less frequently. She allowed him to hold the glass to her trembling lips, to enclose her feeble hands with his because they both knew she'd drop the glass otherwise.

The brandy silked a warm and beguiling path to her stomach and revived her. She kept her gaze fixed on the glass. On his hands. She'd always loved them. Big and capable but with long, slender fingers that had lain against her face while his mouth had slowly descended in a sweet or sometimes blistering kiss… She choked.

'Just drink,' he husked. 'Don't think about anything. Don't torture yourself. It's all right. Honestly.'

But it wasn't. And the sooner she accepted that the better. Though she couldn't help grieving.

'How is it all right?' she whispered mournfully, her voice cracking midway.

He swallowed, some unknown emotion overcoming him. 'It is. Believe me. We'll sort this out. I can't bear to see you so upset,' he husked.

'You should have thought of that before you played hunt the dolly-bird,' she muttered.

His mouth clammed up and he stalked over to shed the towel and grab his robe, turning around once he'd drawn it around his nakedness and had begun to yank the belt into an angrily tied knot.

'You know how hard I've been working!' he lashed. 'I'm not Superman. I would never have had the energy for a dolly-bird!'

She fell silent. Energy could always be found for the things one wanted to do. And he'd proved a moment ago that his sex drive was still active.

He stood there, brooding, dark eyes narrowed and hostile.

'I need you to be calm,' he said flatly.

Her eyes silvered and she averted her head again. Calm? Yes, she was—but only because she felt numb with cold, as if the blood had stopped bothering to do the trip around her body.

She shivered and slid further under the bedclothes, suddenly scared of hearing some trumped-up explanation that had so many holes in it she'd be sieving out the lies for days to come.

'Superficially I am,' she replied in stilted tones. 'But don't let that fool you. Go on. Let's have your explanation.'

Dan inhaled long and hard. 'I can't talk to the back of your head.'

Sullenly she turned over and glued her eyes to the ceiling, her body a taut mass of terror.

'Get on with it,' she whispered.

'Give me a break!' he protested.

'Why?' she blurted out.

His hands clawed into fists. 'If you see no reason, then there isn't much hope for us, is there?'

After that bitter statement, there was a long and painful pause. A sickening atmosphere of hate and suspicion thickened the air between them. She could feel Dan mentally leaving her, the bonds being severed. Despair entered every corner of her heart.

It was incomprehensible to her that he was angry. Surely he realised she was all but dying inside?

'Tell me,' she said in a flat monotone.

He was silent for a few seconds. 'To my mind, it's perfectly simple,' he began eventually, so quietly that she had to strain her utmost to hear. 'I've worked it out. I think that Celine had been planning this for a while.'

'Sex in our home?' she shot miserably before she could stop herself. 'It's the crowning triumph, isn't it?' she cried, more unhappy than she could ever have imagined. She glared at him. 'Like a dog marking a tree on another dog's territory!'

Oh, God! she thought. What awful things was she coming out with?

Dan winced. 'You're overwrought. Don't say things you'll regret—'

'I'm not going to make this easy for you!' she cried, her eyes huge in their hopelessness.

Dan muttered under his breath and bowed his head. Buried his face in his hands. He who had always been invincible. Her rock. She was still finding that she couldn't cope with his distress. It was worse than her own.

What did that mean? she wondered. That she still loved him enough to forgive him? Would she have him back if he begged? Could she ever let him come near her again without thinking of that woman?

'I can't cope with your hatred,' he whispered rawly.

An incredible agony ripped through her flesh, tearing her nerves into ragged strings. And she could not stop shaking, misery and sickness forcing their way up till she had to repeatedly swallow them back down.

He'd been rejected all his life. In his own mind he must see this as yet another rejection. But what did he expect, when he'd behaved so badly? *She* was hurting. *She'd* been wronged.

'Cut out the emotional appeal,' she said jaggedly. 'Give the facts.'

He drew himself up and his hands fell away from his eyes, which he kept lowered to the ground. Helen stared. His dark lashes were wet and glistening. Her gaze flicked to his hands where they lay loosely on his knees and she saw that there was moisture on his fingertips.

But sorrow didn't equal innocence. She steeled herself. And in a halting rasp, he began.

'I had an appointment in Brighton. Celine came, too. Unusually, she brought a flask of coffee.' His mouth took on a harsh line. 'I thought it was an accident, but I can see it wasn't—'

'What was an accident?' she asked in confusion, unnerved by his uncharacteristic rambling. He was always incisive and clear-headed. Or was it her brain that was woolly?

'What? Oh, the coffee. I was driving along and she suddenly poured it out and somehow it spilled all over my shirt and trousers. Black coffee, four sugars, she said. You can't go to the meeting like that, she said. We're near your house. Better go home and change.' He grunted. 'What an idiot I was! Oldest trick in the book.'

Helen waited. He looked sour, as if it had truly happened that way. And she could almost believe that it had...

Except for the abandoned clothes on the stairs, and Celine's implication that this wasn't the first time they'd had 'fun' together. Her head drummed with the questions he wasn't answering.

'And?' she prompted dully.

'We were running late. It was an important meeting and I was annoyed,' Dan growled, his hands doubled into tight fists again. 'I left Celine in the drawing room with a pile of magazines, stormed up the stairs, got out of my ruined clothes—'

'Where are they?' Helen asked suspiciously.

Dan frowned, his eyes flicking up to meet hers. 'What?'

She felt her stomach loop the loop.

'They weren't in the bathroom or I'd have noticed—'

'I left them on top of the laundry basket,' he answered with convincing confidence.

They both looked. The basket sat in pristine solitude in the corner of the bedroom. Dan muttered something rude and strode over to lift the lid but his movements were already uncertain.

'Well?'

Helen could hardly breathe. She wanted them to be there, for some part of his story to be true. Her desperate hope was that he'd stuck to the facts so far—that there *had* been an accident, and Celine had taken the opportunity to wander in while he was half dressed—and had come on so strong that no red-blooded man could have refused—

Dan's expression destroyed her hopes. She flinched, a hollow sensation gnawing at her stomach. His lie had been found out.

'My clothes aren't there,' he announced, his eyes burning feverishly in his face.

'No,' she said, her tone clipped and glacial as she watched him grimly flinging open wardrobe doors and hunting through drawers. 'I never thought they would be.'

'They were!' he insisted, flashing her an irritated glance.

This was awful, she thought as he pretended to search for his supposedly stained clothes. He was making a good job of it, becoming more and more incensed and baffled as he explored every possible hiding place in the room.

'Stop this,' she said wearily. 'I'm not impressed.'

He whirled, hot anger turning his eyes to glittering jet.

His legs were planted apart, his entire body fired with suppressed fury. Helen gulped. He was beginning to believe his own lies, she thought, aghast.

'Just listen to me,' he hissed through his clenched teeth. 'My clothes were splashed with coffee. I put them on the basket and went to take a shower—'

'While Celine silently dashed up the stairs, grabbed your suit and shirt, stuffed them down her cleavage and then raced downstairs to hide them—only to lay a trail of clothes as she came back up again!' she suggested sarcastically.

'Yes! Something like that!'

'Oh, come on, Dan!' she scoffed.

His hand mussed his hair. 'I *know* it sounds mad—'

'Not mad. Preposterous,' she said coldly.

'Well, I don't know how she did it...' Dan continued to thrust an exasperated hand into his hair till it was as confused as his manner. 'All I do know is that I came out of the shower to find Celine wearing nothing but that blue towel.'

That part could be true, she thought grudgingly. Before she'd left for work, she'd taken a fresh one out of the airing cupboard on the landing and had flung it on a bedroom chair ready for her shower later that evening.

'And?' she muttered, not sure she wanted to hear the rest.

He made an impatient gesture with his hand. 'What do you think? I asked her what the hell she was doing, of course.'

'And?' Helen goaded. 'What happened then?'

Dan's eyes blazed at her temerity. 'And nothing!'

'I mean, what reason did she give for stripping off without any encouragement from you?' she persisted.

A frown pulled his brows together. He appeared to be taking a while to think of an answer.

'As a matter of fact, she seemed disconcerted at first, as if she hadn't expected me to find her there—'

'That doesn't make sense.'

'I know! Don't ask me to read the damn woman's mind!' he snapped irascibly. 'I employ her because she's got a brilliant imagination and can think around corners. I'm the straightforward sort.'

'Well, I'm a woman with the same talents as Celine,' she said, 'so let's see if I can unravel the mystery. She deliberately threw the coffee over you, waited downstairs till you went up for your shower and then she stripped. After that, she went up the stairs arranging her things enticingly in reverse order, and slipped into our bedroom to take your suit away—perhaps to send it to the cleaners, like a good PA should,' she suggested acidly. Dan glowered. 'But you came out too soon and caught her snitching my towel, whereas her real plan was that you'd follow the trail of clothes down the stairs, getting progressively more and more excited. And she'd be reclining in a seductive pose on a rug, with a glass of champagne in her hand, a rose in her teeth and a huge smile of welcome on her face.'

He stared, appalled. 'Do you really think—?'

'For heaven's *sake*, Dan!' she scathed. 'Can't you recognise sarcasm?'

Two high spots of colour fired his cheekbones. 'Well, women can be unbelievably devious,' he said angrily. 'I'm beginning to discover that to my cost. I can only give you my version.'

'Which is?' Helen asked, sweetly saccharine.

'I came out of the shower and saw her. When she recovered her composure she just started talking in this odd, husky kind of voice. Saying that this was our opportunity. Stuff like that,' he mumbled.

'Details,' she demanded.

'No.'

'Can't think of any?' she taunted.

He glared. 'It was embarrassing.'

'So relive it.'

'It…was all about her feelings for me. The kind of man she thought I was,' he said shortly. 'I told her not to be so stupid and to get dressed.'

He was lying. He looked ashamed of himself. She would have preferred him to admit his adultery and to beg her forgiveness. This was just cowardly.

'So you're saying that you were confronted with a gorgeous, almost-naked woman who admitted that she worshipped the ground you walked on and said, "How about it?" and you said, "No, thanks, I'm married."'

Dan's astonished indignation was masterly. 'Of course!'

'You're a saint among men.'

'Don't be sarky!' he said angrily, his brows lowered over glittering eyes. 'There's no point in talking to you if you're not going to listen—'

'Oh, I'm listening, Dan,' she replied despondently. 'I'm just sickened by what I'm hearing.'

He slung her a furious glare as if she was doing him an injustice. Past experience told her that this kind of reaction was common when people were in the wrong. They dealt with their fall from grace by seeking excuses for their behaviour, or finding fault with the accuser. It was the only way they could live with themselves.

'If you ask me,' she said coldly, 'you're lucky you're not splattered all over the wall.'

Rage crackled in his eyes. 'That's it. I'm going. You're not prepared to believe me—'

'You're giving up?' she cried, sitting bolt upright, her whole body taut with outrage. He wasn't walking out on her! Not till he'd been forced to tell the truth. 'Don't you have faith in your own story?' she challenged.

'*You* don't. That's the problem.'

He studied her with a chilling coldness. Fear clutched at her heart as she realised that his love had now died. Nothing would resurrect their marriage now. Other than a miracle.

Please let there be one. She couldn't live without Dan. Close to breaking-point, she clasped her trembling hands over her knees, her eyes huge and pleading.

'I want to believe you,' she croaked. 'I honestly do.'

Her words seemed to placate him slightly. The high jut of his shoulders inched down a little.

'OK. I left her in no doubt that I was furious with her. I went back into the bathroom and locked the door to make it clear I wasn't interested. And I waited so she had time to get dressed. Clearly she didn't bother. I assume she heard you and went out onto the landing. When I came out into the bedroom, I heard your voice too and realised you'd come home.'

'That must have been a shock,' she muttered.

'My whole life passed before my eyes,' he admitted grimly. 'When I saw Celine still in that towel, I realised how bad it would look.'

'Bad is an understatement. And you're telling me that I came back just in time to prevent anything taking place?'

'Yes! I mean—no, dammit, I mean nothing *would* have taken place—'

'Supposing I go along with your version. What was her purpose in all this?'

'To get me into bed, I imagine!' he yelled, looking annoyed.

'And yet up to now she hadn't given you the least suspicion that she might be interested in you?'

'No.'

He scowled and thrust his hands into the pockets of his robe aggressively. Even he was seeing that his story was unlikely.

Helen closed her eyes. 'It won't wash, Dan. There are no coffee-stained clothes. And the idea of Celine nipping up and down the stairs like a demented yo-yo is ludicrous.'

'That doesn't make it untrue!' he declared.

She inhaled harshly, stoking up her courage to face the truth and accept it before moving on. Maybe they could pull things together. He could be made to see that you had to be straight with people and earn their love by never letting them down.

'Why don't you admit you've been having an affair,' she said shakily, 'and we can go on from there?'

'Because I haven't! I *wouldn't*!' he seethed, beginning to stride up and down. 'It's the last thing on earth I'd do. You don't really know me at all, do you?'

'No. I don't,' she agreed unhappily, stunned by his air of deep injury.

His shoulders slumped. 'Well, that's crystal-clear. You can't have any idea how much you disappoint me.'

Her mouth opened and closed like a fish coming up for air. '*I* disappoint *you*? How arrogant can you get? You're in the wrong, Dan, and yet you won't unbend your stupid pride and confess! Instead, you come up with a story so weak that it's laughable! I don't believe any part of it!'

'You must!' he warned. 'Or we're finished.'

How dared he issue an ultimatum? Stifling an urge to cry, she fixed him with a steely gaze.

'I'd like to be alone. You'd better use the guest bedroom tonight. Unless, of course,' she added bitterly, her heart one huge ache, 'you prefer to stay at Celine's.'

Dan's mouth tightened into a thin line of anger. 'Thanks for the vote of confidence,' he muttered scathingly, collecting up fresh clothes with feverish haste. 'Nice to know how highly you rate my moral values and my commitment to this marriage.'

Bristling with wounded pride, he spun on his heel and

headed for the door, the ferocity and speed of his stride leaving her in no doubt as to his mood.

After a short while she heard the front door bang, the sound of his car starting up and being wrenched violently into gear. The shriek of wheels spinning on mud. And then a hostile silence.

That was it, she thought bleakly, shocked by the cold reality of his departure. They were enemies now. The end.

CHAPTER FOUR

TO HELEN'S surprise she didn't burst into tears. Perhaps, she thought morosely, that was because her brain had turned to stone and it was incapable of thought any more.

Staying in bed was impossible. Her own restlessness was driving her mad. Desperate to do something, she got up and put on one of Dan's T-shirts and a pair of his walking socks.

They were her comfort clothes, she supposed. She'd often wear them on a Sunday when she allowed herself a precious few hours of leisure.

Perhaps she'd do some housework. Despite not feeling very well, she was too angry to sit still. Cleaning would pass the time and use up some of her suppressed anger as she imposed her will on the hated farmhouse. So she gathered up some cleaning equipment and set to work.

In an odd way, she almost enjoyed the activity, and felt grimly satisfied to see that Dan's study curtains quivered in subdued terror after she'd whacked the dust from them with a table-tennis bat.

'Be afraid,' she muttered, glowering at the rest of his room. 'Be very afraid!' And she cleaned it within an inch of its life.

All of the rooms had borne a sad and neglected air when she'd started. Housework had never been high on her list of priorities because the builders and plasterers kept ruining her efforts.

But by the time she'd polished and dusted and hoovered everything with manic attention to detail, the spiders had fled in shock and each habitable room hummed with the energy she'd expended.

The house almost looked homely, she mused grudgingly and pretended not to notice the deep sob which lurched up from nowhere into her throat.

It was only when she'd cleared rubble and plaster from the builders' latest extension project—ironically the nursery-to-be—that she paused for breath, remembered where she was and suddenly found herself convulsed with weeping.

That was it. She spent a chilly hour in the nursery hunched up in the dust, mournfully twisting the knife into herself by gazing at the place where she'd planned to put the cot and its precious occupant.

The floodgates opened. Her burst of displacement activity was over. Almost too blurred to see through the curtain of tears, she dispiritedly made herself a fresh hot-water bottle and dragged herself up to bed.

Eventually her howling turned to intermittent sobbing and she found herself listening for Dan's car, every sound outside rocketing her hopes up to a peak of anticipation, only for disappointment to follow. Dan didn't come back at all. In her heart of hearts she knew he wouldn't, not with Celine panting eagerly on the sidelines.

Most of the night she spent awake, morbidly cuddling his pillow, reflecting that she'd never been really unhappy before. Unlike Dan, she'd had a childhood unblemished by tragedy or trauma. Her parents—now enjoying life in the Californian sun—adored her. She'd been popular at school and clever enough not to worry about exams.

This feeling of deep misery was totally alien. For the first time she understood what it was like to be unhappy and to lose a person you loved. It was frightening, she mused, to surrender your whole self to someone and to have that commitment flung back in your face as if it were worthless.

She felt as if he'd crushed her. Trampled on her dreams, knocked the confidence out of her. He'd chosen someone else, effectively telling her that she wasn't good enough. So her self-esteem was at an all-time low.

Wearily she crawled out of bed the next morning and rang in sick. All through the day she continued her on-slaught on the house, with frequent breaks for a crying fit whenever she came across something that reminded her of Dan. Which was often. Yet she slogged on with dogged determination.

She still felt sick but she was learning to ignore that. The house needed to be in good shape if it was going to be photographed and put on the market. Tomorrow she'd speak to her solicitor. At the moment she couldn't be sure she wouldn't bawl down the phone. She had her dignity, after all.

Dusk was now falling. She'd been working since dawn, clad as before in Dan's big T-shirt and the cosy socks.

A sudden dizziness made her clutch at the table in the hall that she was polishing. The duster floated to the floor and she stared vacantly into space, weak from her stomach bug, from exhaustion and lack of food.

An eerie silence descended on the house, almost suf-focating her. The loneliness of her situation hit her like a ton of bricks and a sense of hopelessness weighted her down. She was a reject.

Her eyes widened in shock at how deeply Dan had wounded her confidence.

'I'm fabulous!' she told herself with a sniff. 'A catch for any man.'

She wasn't convinced. Desperate to feel better about herself, she found her way to the wine rack in the farm-house kitchen and poured herself a modest measure. Red

wine was good for you, full of iron and things, she thought
vaguely. She relaxed a little as the liquid wound its way
down to her stomach and calmed it.

But she couldn't shut out the thoughts of Dan that were
now crowding her mind, taunting her, slicing her heart
with ruthless precision. So she finished her drink, intending to have another, thinking it might be a good anaesthetic.

Better, she mused, after a sip or two. She might even
be able to sleep now. Her head felt muzzy and she dimly
realised that she hadn't eaten at all that day. Stupid. No
more for her! Time she got horizontal and in bed before
she fell over.

With a sigh, she was about to turn around when she felt
the hair prickling on the back of her neck as if she was
being watched. Very slowly she checked over her shoulder—and her hand went to her pounding heart in relief.

'Dan!' Hastily she turned off the automatically joyous
light in her eyes and fashioned her face into a more appropriate scowl. 'I didn't hear you come in.'

How achingly desirable he looked. An appealing mixture of sleek-suited executive, and open-collared, sexily
askew-tie lover. Someone else's lover, she reminded herself painfully.

And here she was, looking sickly, plain and horribly
scruffy in a T-shirt and socks. Crossly she wished she'd
been draped in something diaphanous and utterly alluring.
She yanked the T-shirt straight and wished she hadn't because it bounced a bit, drawing Dan's piercing gaze to her
naked thighs.

'How are you?' he asked, as stiff and uncompromising
as if his jaw had been turned to granite.

Her head whirled with the effort of thinking.

'Yukky.'

'There's a smell of polish.'

'Diversionary tactic.'

She frowned. Had those words come out right? She'd had to say them very slowly.

'I see.' He licked his lips with the very tip of his tongue, his eyes oddly heavy as he contemplated her. 'I think I could do with a drink,' he muttered.

Loose-limbed and worryingly woozy, she lurched over to reach up for a glass, pushing it and the bottle along the counter top. Dan was far too close, giving off an enticing scent of maleness that made her sway nearer in an attempt to mark that scent in her memory for ever.

'You're back from work early,' she observed, trying not to sound slurred.

Dan nodded curtly. He had no intention of telling her that he hadn't been to work at all, that his entire day had been spent coming to terms with the fact that Helen was like all the others. Not to be entrusted with his feelings.

'Came back to pack some of my stuff,' he replied.

Good. That was virtually emotionless.

His eyes hungered for her, though. She was rosy-cheeked, her gaze languid from the wine. He wondered how much she'd drunk. Her hair had been screwed back in a pony-tail. It looked cute. He liked seeing her face without make-up. Her mouth was naturally red, the upper lip so arched that it made him ache to kiss it.

The T-shirt showed too much of her incomparably long and slender legs. And when she had turned her back to reach for the glass, he'd had an eyeful of the tantalising first curves of two rounded buttocks.

'You're off, then,' she commented with slow care.

'Uh-huh.' He sipped thoughtfully, his eyes narrowed.

It gave him a sexual kick to see her wearing his top. It hung loosely, moulding to her beautiful breasts. Hazarding a guess, he'd say that she wore nothing underneath at all.

But she was taboo now. Still his wife, but only because a piece of paper said so.

A sourness filled his mouth and he drained his glass to mask the taste.

'You look a bit better,' he said, baffled as to why he was indulging in this ludicrous conversation instead of escaping unharmed.

She gave a short 'Huh!' and squinted ruefully down at herself. Her arm described a rather uncontrolled arc in the air before falling to her side. 'Let's be honest. I look a mess.'

There was an awkward pause. Unable to think of anything original to say—or even anything banal—he reached for the bottle just as she did, their hands meeting…and lingering for an electrifying moment.

Oh, hell, he thought, his guts melting. He wanted her.

'After you,' he said, dredging up a grunt.

Her hand was shaking. She slopped wine all over the counter. Blushing beautifully, she reached across to grab a cloth, her mouth so sweetly parted over her even white teeth that he couldn't bear it any longer.

His hand descended on her bare arm. Warm flesh seemed to fuse with his.

'Let me,' he said in a ridiculous husk.

He cleared his throat, hoping she'd imagine he had a cold. Presumably he ought to let go of her. Reluctantly he did so. When he mopped up the wine with an air of concentration, she didn't move back but stayed to tantalise him with enticing drifts of warm woman, polish and soap.

'So,' he said stupidly, bemused by the electrification of his entire nervous system.

This hadn't happened for weeks. Bit late now. He filled her glass and then his for want of something better to do. 'Yes?'

Her voice had quavered. Her lower lip was trembling

and all he could think of was the way it would feel when he took it in his mouth. Fleshy. Yielding. With an inner groan, he took a swig of wine and struggled to add something to the 'so'.

'Uh...I'll go and pack.'

He'd had to drag the words out. What he wanted was to stay here and gaze at her. No. To hold her. Slide his hands beneath the cotton fabric and feel the yielding of her fabulous body. Slowly, thoroughly, make mad, passionate love to her...

'Right.'

Her lashes lay darkly on her cheeks as she took small sips from the glass. There was a softness to her face that he hadn't noticed before—she'd always been thin, with fantastic cheekbones, but now she positively glowed. He liked the way she looked. Womanly. Inviting.

A spasm sucked at his loins. 'Just finish my wine, then.'

He heard the bright, polite and meaningless rubbish he was uttering and tightened his mouth in exasperation. Why couldn't he tell her, show her, how he felt?

He knew the answer to that. In a word: self-preservation. All his life he'd protected himself from others. He'd made an exception in Helen's case, believing she'd never let him down, that they'd be together for ever. Big mistake.

'There's stuff of yours in the tumble-drier,' she said.

Graceful as ever, she put her glass down with exaggerated care and physically pointed herself at the utility room.

It was then that he knew she was a bit squiffy. And it only took a slight and wicked adjustment of his balance for her to blunder into him.

'Oh, whoops!' she gurgled in surprise.

His hands eagerly went out to steady her. *What was he doing?*

'Sorry. My fault,' he said, releasing her with a supreme act of will.

'No. Mine.'

Definitely slurred. She didn't move. There was something painfully forlorn about her whole attitude. Without another thought in his head, he took her in his arms and drew her close, just holding her to his chest.

It was natural that she'd be upset and lost. They'd known each other since she was fourteen. Parting would be…

He stopped thinking about it. It hurt too much.

'You'll be OK,' he assured her curtly.

She was tough. Sailed through life with her amusing quips that made him laugh like a drain and a swift application of her sharp brain that impressed him like hell. God, he'd envied her. Nothing had ever scarred her. Nobody had ever made her feel she was unwanted or a waste of space.

Total self-assurance ran through to her very core. She'd soon be snapped up by someone else…

No!

In a violent blur of anger and lurching emotion, he roughly tipped up her chin and kissed her fiercely on her open lips, pulling her against his painfully aroused body.

He felt her shock, the deep shudder that ran through her. Loath to hang around where he wasn't wanted, he was about to release her when he felt her hands slide up his chest and lodge awkwardly in the gaps between his shirt buttons. One of her favourite moves.

Soon she'd tease the buttons free and nuzzle him with her nose and mouth, teeth and tongue. A jerk of longing arced through his body. Knowing he was mad to play with fire, he groaned and let his kiss become slower, gentler, more exploratory.

His intention then was to step away and say farewell, but the road to Hell was paved with intentions, wasn't it?

Because she wasn't having any of this friendly goodbye. It seemed she wanted fire and passion because her mouth drove hard into his and her hands were pulling at his clothes frenetically.

Something snapped inside him. In a blind fog he gently lifted her onto the counter top, one hand hooked behind her head so that their mouths continued their bruising kisses and the other sliding up beneath her top to settle beneath one heavy breast.

His eyes closed in agonised bliss. As always, it felt incredibly voluptuous, swollen and hot. He had to get her T-shirt off. Impatiently he dragged it up and let her take over.

For a moment her body stretched up, lithe, shapely, and staggeringly erotic with her gorgeous breasts lifted high and her arms reaching above her head as she wriggled out of the top. He was shaking, marvelling at the huge plum centres, peaking for him, enticing his mouth...

And she was sweet to taste. Her nipples shaped to his lips as he suckled greedily and she grabbed his hair, moaning. Beneath his hands her skin felt beautifully smooth as if it was straining to contain her flesh. The sensations were so intense that he felt drunk with them, so drunk that he could hardly stand.

His nose burrowed into the firmness of her, inhaling the unique fragrance of her body as he worshipped every inch of her deeply sensual breasts.

But she was in a hurry. His scalp tingled where she'd tugged fistfuls of hair, his face burned from her scalding, desperate kisses and grazing teeth, which were now nipping his lower lip urgently. Every last corner of his head was filled with their laboured breathing, his mind just a mass of cataclysmic connections that fired his pleasure centres and nothing else.

Her hand enclosed his and drew it from where it was enjoying the lengthening of one rosy nipple. About to protest, he let out a guttural groan instead as he felt the warmth of her thighs and then her wetness waiting for him.

His head spinning, he managed to put his hands on her waist and to lift her. With Helen's legs wrapped around him, he staggered more by luck than judgement to the adjoining sitting room, kissing her deeply and with mounting hunger as she writhed and squirmed against his body.

He laid her down on the carpet and tore at his own clothes with the impatience of a teenage boy. Her hair was falling about her face, the band holding it hastily ripped off. They stared at one another with naked need and as his nudity increased her eyes became more and more sultry, her lips more inviting and his heart came close to bursting.

She didn't want a long, slow seduction. And he too was enveloped in a sense of desperation, some part of his non-functioning brain retaining the knowledge that this would be the last time he ever made love to his wife.

Although he was tender with her as always, their lovemaking had a different dimension. He had never known her to be so uninhibited, so intensely passionate and fierce. She blew his mind away, every stroke of his body stoking up the furnaces that inflamed his nerves, every touch and caress affecting him like wildfire. They were both crying out and shouting, their bodies moving with exquisite perfection, drawing the very last ounce of sensation from their union.

Through the misty haze that covered his eyes he saw that she was more beautiful than he had ever remembered. Sweat-licked, carnally erotic, she lured him on with her eyes, mouth, her hands and her entire body till every sense he possessed went into meltdown.

His body flamed like a furnace. Exquisite pain tore at his sensitised nerves. He couldn't bear it. No more, please, it was so good, too good...

Shellbursts of pleasure. And again. And yet again...

He couldn't breathe. He seemed to be balancing on a summit, every muscle in his body tightened so fiercely that he ached everywhere. And then gradually consciousness began to flood back, his jerking muscles relaxed and he floated back to earth again.

Back to a whole raft of guilt and regret for what he'd done.

Helen lay limply beneath him, her eyes closed, a blissful smile on her lips. Gently he pushed the hair from her flushed face.

'Helen.'

She didn't stir. Moving carefully, so he didn't disturb her, he shifted his weight and just gave himself up to luxuriating in the extraordinary tremors chasing through the cells of his body.

He swallowed as a terrible emotion welled up inside him. It was pushing away the barriers he'd painstakingly erected and it threatened to flood his entire being with a destructive weakness.

'Helen!' he whispered, checking.

Deep asleep. He was glad. He had to grab a shower, chuck some clothes on fast...

And then he must ring Celine.

Helen stretched languorously and reached out automatically for Dan. To her surprise her hands encountered nothing but the fibres of the carpet. Reluctantly her eyes peeled open.

For a moment she lay there, dismay seeping into her

very bones as she realised two things. They had made love—mind-blowing, unbelievable love that had shot her up into the stratosphere somewhere—and he had gone.

Another thought sneaked into her confused mind. Where had he learnt to touch a woman like that? It had always been good, but never so…

She blushed scarlet, feeling the heat rippling through her turgid body, arousing it again. With disgust, she crushed her lust. Blanked out as well as she could the memory of Dan's desire-filled eyes luring her on, the intensity of his passion and the terrible need he had satisfied in her.

How could she have been so stupid? He'd probably packed his clothes and scooted off, vastly amused that she'd been so pie-eyed from drinking on an empty stomach that she'd given him a good time as a parting gesture!

Furious with herself, she crawled dazedly to her feet, aching and tender from the most tenderly impassioned seduction she'd ever known. Or would ever know, she decided gloomily.

And she'd willingly encouraged him.

The starkness of her nudity was mortifying. She'd been…*outrageous*. All that yelling and urging… It was as if she'd been desperate to be loved by him one last time. Though love hadn't come into it. Dan had just reacted like any man with sex uppermost in his mind.

Feeling vulnerable in the middle of the sitting room, she wrapped her arms around herself and wondered what to do.

She couldn't face the stairs. Not so soon after Dan's highly physical goodbye and with the memory of Celine's pink briefs haunting every step.

There was a shower in the downstairs cloakroom. She'd use that, then find the T-shirt. Scarlet shame invaded her body from the feet up. She seemed to remember she'd whirled her top over her head and lobbed it in the direction of the pasta jar.

Nervously she crept to the door, listened, and began to cross the hall. Halfway, with her arms wrapped around herself to protect her modesty, she suddenly froze.

Dan was still in the house—and talking to someone in the study.

'Celine!' she muttered under her breath, hoping beyond hope that it wasn't.

Grimly determined to investigate, Helen tiptoed to the shower and grabbed a bath sheet. Her heart thumped so loudly she thought he must hear it. Stealthily she padded over to the study and put her ear to the door.

'Thank God you're there!' she heard him exclaim with huge relief. And passionately he added, 'I need to see you. I've *got* to talk to you, Celine!'

'*Oh-h-h!*'

Unable to believe his nerve, she hurled the door open with such force that it smashed against the wall and rebounded. Dan dropped the phone in shock. Like a whirlwind she ran forwards and slammed it back in its cradle, exploding with a monumental fury.

'You two-timing, selfish, deceitful, scum of the earth!' she yelled, barely two inches from him, her body quivering, almost bouncing, with incandescent rage. 'You disgust me! You're…obscene!' she spluttered. 'How dare you take advantage of me? You must have known I'd had too much to drink! And now you're ringing *her!*'

She was beginning to sob out the words, distraught that their love-making had been nothing special to him at all. When it had touched the very depths of her soul.

'I will never, ever, speak to you again!' she cried vehemently. 'You'll contact me through my solicitor…' She found herself unable to construct a sentence. 'Get divorce. Contemptible! Broken trust…amoral, vile…'

Now she was incoherent, words just emerging wildly, arms windmilling in all directions. But he did nothing, just stayed where he was, impassive, cold, utterly closed to her.

Her head buzzed strangely. Something black seemed to roll across her eyes and the last thing she knew was that she was falling into a deep and endless well of nothing.

The blackness became grey and then she was being dragged unwillingly into daylight. No—the glow of a lamp. Blinking, she discovered that she was in bed. Naked. Waves of sickness were coursing through her and she scrambled miserably for the bathroom where she retched emptily.

Dan came into the room as she was wearily climbing back between the sheets. In hip-hugging jeans and casual T-shirt he looked undeniably sexy. And also quite appalled.

'Helen!'

Dan wet his dry lips with a deliberate thoroughness and she stiffened. There must be a reason why he was shaking, why the steaming mug in his hand was slopping hot liquid onto his hand—and yet he wasn't even wincing.

Warily she sat up, hugging the sheet to her body, her grey eyes huge with alarm.

'What?' she breathed.

The mug was placed on the bedside table. Dan kept staring at her helplessly, his hands now thrust into his pockets, and he swallowed several times before he managed to speak again.

'You...fainted.'

She glowered, bristling. 'I certainly did. I hope you realise how much you've hurt me.'

'There's a problem.' He seemed unsure how to go on.

'All of your making,' she muttered.

'No...you...keep feeling sick.'

She furled her brow. 'So?'

Dan sucked in a huge breath and strode about the room erratically while Helen watched him in amazement. He was so rigid he looked as if he might snap. Each jerky step jarred his entire body, sending ripples of movement across the straining T-shirt and his grim, flinty face.

Suddenly he whipped around, his bulk silhouetted against the window so that she couldn't make out his expression.

'Your body's changed. It *feels* different.'

Cut to the quick, she flushed and ensured that the sheet stayed up around her neck in concealment.

'Do you mean I'm fat?' she demanded icily.

'No...I don't know, but it *is* different—'

'Oh. Texture? Firmness? Different to Celine's? Well,' she hurtled on before he had a chance to reply, 'maybe it's because I rarely have time to eat a proper meal nowadays. I'm snatching things on the run. Doughnuts. French fries. Bars of chocolate. Anyway,' she went on, determined not to be crushed by him, 'I like the way I am. And you didn't seem to mind too much just now!'

That hit home. She knew she'd wounded him when he took a step back and rocked on his heels. But she didn't like what she'd done.

'I'm sorry,' she said, lowering her eyes in shame. 'I don't know why I said that. I couldn't help it. But you must realise I've reason to be upset. And I feel so grungy with this wretched gastric thing—'

'I don't think it's that, Helen,' he said carefully. 'There could be another reason why you're being sick.'

'What?'

He just stared. Gradually the weight of his words suddenly sank into her. She went very still, as if all life in her body had been suspended, her eyes enormous in her pale face.

No. She couldn't be.

Not...*pregnant*!

CHAPTER FIVE

'I—I'M JUST…sick,' Helen protested in a small, frightened voice. 'One of those tummy bugs. I'll get better in a day or so.'

A spasm pinched Dan's mouth in. He seemed to be struggling with the fear that they might have created a baby just when their marriage was falling apart. Help us all! she thought. That would be so hard to bear! What incredibly awful timing! The poor little baby…

Hoarsely he croaked, 'You're saying it's not possible?'

'No…I…'

Helen chewed her lip, aghast. She cast her mind around, trying to remember when she'd last had a period. Life had been so hectic that she'd lost track. It must have been ages.

'I'm sure it's unlikely. After all, we haven't been near each other for weeks,' she dissembled sullenly.

'But you could be,' Dan persisted, his brooding eyes and harsh tone unnerving her.

'I don't *know*!'

Impatience swept across his features. 'Surely you keep a record of dates?' he asked coldly.

Her throat tightened. Being pregnant right now would be an absolute disaster. This was the worst possible time that it could have happened. She could see that he was horrified by the idea. And the last thing she wanted was to be a single mother, struggling on her own…

'In my bag. Diary,' she choked. The collapse of her dreams was complete.

Wordlessly he handed it to her, his hand shaking. She

61

glanced up and felt herself shrivel under his ferocious expression. He was incredibly angry. As if it was her fault!

'There's no point in getting annoyed with me,' she snapped, her hands plucking aimlessly at the counterpane and betraying her inner turmoil.

'Just look, will you?' he ordered, unnervingly close to erupting.

All fingers and thumbs, she rummaged in the roomy bag. How had it come to this? A few days ago they would have been anxious at the thought that she might be pregnant, a little shocked, but…eventually thrilled.

Instead, she wasn't sure how she felt. And Dan was holding back a monumental fury with great difficulty, presumably irritated that he might be saddled with maintenance for a child he didn't want, for a woman he didn't love.

She couldn't be pregnant. Mustn't be. Not with Dan so hostile to the idea.

'I've found it.'

Opening the small leather book, she stared for several seconds at the calendar with its increasingly haphazard marks, trying to make sense of what it was telling her.

'Well?' demanded Dan.

Her brain shut down for a moment as shock waves rocketed through it. Muttering an expletive under his breath, he came forward and snatched the book from her, scowling at the page as if it might as well have been in Sanskrit.

'What's this mean?' He thrust the book back at her. 'It doesn't have any pattern to it.'

'I-I've been irregular for ages.' Panic raced through her brain, helping her to invent explanations. 'That can happen, you know. Stressed lifestyle and a poor diet—'

'All I need to know is, when was your last period?' he asked heavily, cutting short her frantic excuses.

Her eyes rounded with apprehension as she met his stony stare. 'Uh…April twenty-third,' she squeaked.

Dan whisked in a sharp breath and sat down on the bed as if his legs had crumpled beneath him.

'My birthday was on May seventh,' he said abruptly.

She knew what he was suggesting. They'd celebrated with a rare meal out in London and had come home feeling so happy to have been together that they'd made love the minute they'd got home. And several times more.

Oh, heck. Now what? Fretting, she knew she couldn't remain in bed a moment longer. She needed to do something. Catch up with the ironing. Dig the garden…

'I need a shower,' she muttered, scrambling up and heading blindly for the bathroom, tears falling down her wan face.

'A…*shower*? *Now*?' he gasped.

'Not a crime!' she hurled back and ran in, wrenching the lever of the power shower to its limit before he could catch up with her.

She welcomed the battering, taking it as her punishment for being so stupid as to allow him to make love to her despite his infidelity, for not noticing her periods had stopped, for being trusting and naive when everyone knew that if you took your eyes off a man for a second he'd be chatting up someone else.

Muttering under her breath about her rank idiocy, she scrubbed all trace of Dan from her body. It hurt. Outside and within her heart. But now she was free of him. All traces erased.

Bereft, she gave a broken sob and penalised herself by massaging shampoo into her hair with hard and ruthless fingers, before sluicing off the soap.

The thundering water ceased as if by magic. Pink and tingling from every pore, Helen warily eyed a partly drenched Dan, whose gaze was slowly raking over her, the T-shirt clinging wetly to his magnificent torso.

The tips of her breasts jerked into life. Heat curled seductively in a pool somewhere within her body and Dan's eyes flickered.

'Get out,' he muttered, permafrost in his expression. 'We have things to discuss. You can't just walk away—'

'I badly needed a shower. I felt dirty,' she defended haughtily, collecting her thick, fluffy blue robe and slipping into it.

The sensuality of her reaction to him had shaken her. Must be some kind of latent memory, she thought crossly, drying her legs with ruthless vigour. It was about time her body came up to speed and recognised him as a danger to her health and sanity.

The permafrost deepened. 'You pick your moments,' he commented.

Winding a towel around her dripping hair, she saw that water was dripping from him.

'You're drenched,' she said unnecessarily.

'And you're avoiding the issue.'

'There is no issue. It's ridiculous,' she scorned, rubbing at her hair and wincing. Her scalp must be scarlet, she thought and struggled back to the argument. 'I take the pill,' she declared firmly. 'We agreed, we didn't want children for a while. We intended to work hard and provide a solid, stable b-background…'

Her voice tailed off in a little wobble. So much for that idea. Their plans had been hijacked by Dan's infidelity.

'No method is infallible,' he pointed out with maddening truth. 'And at the beginning of April you were on antibiotics for a sore throat, remember? Didn't I read somewhere that they affect the pill?'

But that couldn't happen to her. They'd been so careful, made sensible plans…

'Dan, I can't be pregnant!' she insisted in mounting alarm. 'I'd be…' She ran back into the bedroom and picked up her diary. With a shaking finger she totted up the weeks. No. It wasn't possible. Her pulses steadied. 'Over two *months*!' she cried, when he followed her in. 'How could I not know about that? Women have an intuition about these things—'

'Have you had any *time* for intuition?' he asked quietly.

She went white in the middle of rough-drying her hair. 'Not so's you'd notice,' she admitted.

Feeling jittery, she abandoned her hair and stalked into the bedroom to grab some clothes, nervous at being watched so intently by the menacing Dan. He had stripped off his top and was slowly rubbing his chest dry, his eyes unsmiling and unnervingly bleak.

'It's been as much as I could do to keep on top of work and the sheer day-to-day survival,' she mumbled, hopping her way into a pair of white briefs.

'Well, think about it now,' he muttered shortly, finding himself a clean shirt and dragging it on with angry, hasty hands. '*Intuit.* How do you feel?'

After shooting him a glare, she let her hand rest on her stomach. Was it her imagination, or had it rounded significantly? The skin did seem taut…kind of shiny… Her huge eyes met his.

'Gungy. Funny—'

'What sort of funny?' he pounced.

'I don't know, do I? I don't feel…myself. As if…as if…'

'As if you're pregnant,' he supplied, snapping out the words in contempt of her stupidity at monitoring her own body.

Hastily she covered herself up with a shirt and heaved on her jeans. 'There!' she declared. 'I can do them up. I can't be pregnant.'

'You've been sick,' he pointed out. 'You've hardly eaten anything. The two could have cancelled each other out.'

'So you're an instant expert on pregnancy now?' she snapped. 'I admit, I'm probably run down and anaemic—'

'With all the signs of early pregnancy,' Dan said remorselessly, his arms folded in a belligerent attitude.

Helen flushed with resentment, puzzled by his fierce interrogation. 'Don't go on at me!' she cried, feeling suddenly emotional.

'You cry more than you used to,' he observed coldly as a tear trailed a shiny path down the side of her nose.

'I've more reason to!' she yelled.

'Keep calm!' he barked. 'If you *are* pregnant, you need to change your way of life.'

'Typical!' she snorted. 'I have to start wearing pink gingham and drinking lemonade and smile sweetly all day long, while you swan about swashbuckling your way through life as usual!'

'I don't swashbuckle. I work darn hard. And whatever you say, you can't continue with your current job,' he said obstinately. 'Your schedule is so hectic that you'd put my child's life at risk, and I won't have that!'

'It's my child, too!' she pointed out heatedly. 'And I'm certainly not mooning around waiting to give birth. I need to earn a living if I'm to provide for *my* child—'

'You don't know you *have* a child yet,' he reminded her grimly.

'Oh. No.'

Deflated by that possibility, she felt confused and uncertain whether she welcomed the idea or not, now. Practically speaking, it would be a nightmare. But…something undeniably maternal was tugging at her heartstrings, whispering seductively that a baby would be wonderful.

It was just the wrong time. When she was ready, she

wanted a *proper* family: husband, child or children—the whole package. The whole point of having a baby was to share it with someone you loved. To coo over it together, watch it learn to toddle and speak, to play daft games and make sandcastles...

Her body drooped with the realisation that it could be years before she met someone as special as Dan. And she'd be old and grey by then and they'd have to try IVF—

'Your shirt's done up all wrong,' Dan said huskily.

Hormones, or something deep and needy, made her heart leap. With smoky eyes she gazed at him in puzzled confusion. He was moving towards her. Reaching out a hand. Undoing the buttons.

The nerves in her body screamed at her. It had been a mistake to meet his black molasses eyes. She was beginning to drown in their hauntingly unfathomable depths and now the soft sultriness of his achingly sensual mouth was weakening her will and melting all her defences.

Slowly she raised her hand. And miraculously stopped him.

'I can do it,' she breathed, shocked to find how ragged she sounded, how rapidly her chest was rising and falling. She had to rebuff him. She knew that look of his. It was stark-naked carnality.

And she ached to be in his arms again, to know that new and exhilarating sensation of their recent love-making, which had teetered precariously on the edge of desperation. But for her own sanity she must get a grip.

Something in her eyes must have alerted him of her decision to stay aloof.

'Go on, then, do it,' he challenged, remaining whisper-close, mind-numbingly desirable.

Of course she fumbled. Made a hash of it. Got hot and

bothered while he stood there, exuding male pheromones that were sending her crazy, her entire body liquid for him.

'There,' she said shakily, standing her ground. 'Dan, you've got to stop making passes at me. It's over.'

'Is it?' he asked hoarsely.

Her eyes virtually crackled with anger. 'Yes! You know it is!'

'Then how do you explain what keeps happening between us?' he growled.

'I can't answer for you. But my mind is clear, it's just my body that's still working in the past. It'll soon get the message. I don't like responding to you. It's a knee-jerk reaction, nothing else—and I find your groping absolutely *intolerable*! Now. Where were we?'

Dark eyes regarded her with a suddenly harsh contemplation.

'Trying to discover whether you are pregnant,' he clipped. 'How much did you drink this evening?'

Too much, she thought gloomily. And then her eyes widened in alarm.

'One small glass, a few sips of another… Dan! If I am pregnant, could that—?' Her voice dried up.

'I'm sure that's all right. It's nothing,' he said gruffly.

'And…' Her hands twisted anxiously, a terrible fear making her heart rate quicken. 'We…' She checked herself. It would be a travesty to say they'd made love. 'We had sex! If—if we've endangered the baby and I have a miscarriage I'll never, ever forgive you!' she wailed.

There was a deathly silence following her outburst, broken only by their harsh breathing. Then uncertainly he said, 'I didn't fling you around. I was gentle, wasn't I? I'm sure sex is all right—'

'You would say that!' she jerked. 'If I am pregnant, I don't want it to die inside me because you couldn't keep your hands to yourself!'

'That's *cruel*, Helen!' he objected savagely, his face pinched and white with shock.

'It's how I feel!' she sobbed. And was instantly distressed by what she'd said. 'Oh, I'm sorry, I'm *sorry*.'

'Hell. So am I. We were both responsible for what happened,' he growled.

She covered her face with her hands and faced the frightening truth. 'Yes,' she admitted with a sniff. Tear-stained and vulnerable, she lifted her head and caught a look of agony in his eyes. 'I accept responsibility, too,' she said shakily. 'Oh, Dan, what are we going to do if the worst happens? How will we ever be able to forgive ourselves and I have a baby…and it's harmed?'

'There's no point in crossing bridges before we come to them. The first thing to do is to find out one way or the other,' he said almost gently. 'I'll make you an appointment with the doctor.'

'No…' She groaned. She didn't want to know. 'We don't have one,' she remembered with relief. 'I'll get one of those test things.'

'You've still got to see a doc,' he pointed out. 'There's one in the village a mile away. I've noticed the brass plate on the gatepost when I've driven past.'

'I don't want to go.' Her eyes pleaded to be let off.

'You must!' he insisted. 'We both need to know the situation.'

The corners of her mouth drooped. She knew he was right but that didn't make it any easier.

'Dan,' she mumbled feebly. 'I'm *scared*.'

His eyes were unreadable. For a second or two he stared at her trembling figure. Then he shrugged.

'Nothing either of us can do, is there?'

Irrational still, she wanted to be taken in his arms and reassured, to be promised that they'd stick together and he was sorry, desperately sorry he'd cheated on her. If only he'd do that, she thought miserably, she'd accept that he'd strayed because he'd felt unloved and that he'd lacked affection.

They'd both made a mistake, thinking their love could weather any crisis. They'd been wrong. It needed nurturing, not neglect.

Too late, she thought unhappily. Her spiky lashes fluttered as she struggled to hold back the tears.

'What are we going to do if I am?' she jerked.

Every muscle in his body went rigid. 'That's your own affair. All I ask is that you let me have access.'

It was a flat statement, without emotion. Helen was too appalled to speak. It was as if he were talking about sharing one of their favourite videos.

Her body still throbbed from their love-making. Sex, she corrected. And yet he'd phoned his mistress straight after—and now they were coldly discussing access arrangements for a child that might not even exist!

'I despise you!' she hissed, feeling hysterical. Her spirits sank. *Was* that her hormones playing her up? She tried to flatten her voice, to sound more rational despite the deep hurt that was making her heart huge and aching as if it had been bruised and was swollen to twice its size. 'I want you out of my life. As from now.'

'Oh, no, you don't. I'm coming with you to the doctor's. I want to hear what he has to say. If you're pregnant then I want to know. *Then* I'll get out of your life. After that, I'll only appear to see my child.'

'Then for both our sakes,' she flared, distraught that he was abandoning her, 'I hope I've got some virus! Something minor, like E.coli! Or—or malaria! The last thing I want is to keep seeing you on a regular basis!'

He flinched. 'Mutual,' he snarled, and spun on his heel in a filthy temper. 'I'll make the appointment,' he flung brusquely over a high shoulder as he disappeared through the doorway. 'I'll collect my things some time later, when you're not around, and I'll ring you with the appointment time and meet you there.'

He turned around suddenly. Helen's eyes widened. His brows were lowered over glittering black eyes, his mouth a hard and uncompromising line. Every inch of his body quivered with a barely contained rage.

'Be there!' he shot in grim warning. 'Or I'll come and get you, even if I have to bind and gag you and carry you into the surgery over my shoulder. And don't even *think* about disappearing off the face of the earth. I'd find you. Make no mistake about that!'

Dragging in a strangled breath, she watched him stride out of the room and listened to his pounding feet as he thundered down the stairs, two, three at a time.

For a moment she was rooted to the spot. Then, overwhelmed by an urge to see him leave, she ran to the window. The security light came on outside, turning the rain into silver stair-rods, and her heartbeat accelerated while she strained for a glimpse of him.

Disappointingly, a big golfing umbrella restricted her view to his boots and the lower half of his body as he forged his way across the muddy ground to his car. She tried to fill in the rest and found herself sentimentally mooning over every detail of his features: the way he smiled, that dear little squiggle thing he did with his eyebrow...

'I love you, Dan!' she breathed, horribly confused by her see-saw emotions. She hated him. Loved him. Oh, yes. That was the truth of it. Whether he was a deceiver or not, her heart was inextricably entwined with Dan's. She'd given it to him long ago and that was where it seemed to want to stay. 'Why did you do this to me? I need you so badly...'

Braving the stinging rain, she opened the window to

call to him. But to her utter frustration, the wind swept away her choking cries and Dan was clearly far too intent on hurrying to sexpot Celine and her exciting pink underwear with its cute fringes to bother to look back at the boring wife he'd so cruelly betrayed.

Realising her efforts were to no avail, she shut the window and stood shivering, inflicting self-torture by making herself witness the last moments of her husband's departure.

The headlights of the BMW lit up the barn, then swept around to illuminate the mess that was their front garden. All too soon he had vanished from sight.

That was that. She stared into space, grieving for her loss. Only a short time ago she'd been married to a man she loved and admired with all her heart. Now she was left with nothing.

Except, perhaps his baby.

Helen's heart tumbled over and over. She became still. 'Are you in there, baby?' she said experimentally, and moved both hands over her abdomen. A small spark of life rippled through her dulled spirits, lifting them a fraction. 'I'll look after you,' she said, just in case her child felt anxious, in case her distress and the rows with Dan had caused harm. Suddenly a fierce strength poured into her, filling every nerve and fibre of her being. 'I *will* be tough. I won't mope. If you're in there, I promise I'll be a model mother-to-be.' Briefly she let a faint smile lift her sad mouth. 'But I draw the line at pink gingham. OK with you?'

Filled with curiosity she ran to the full-length mirror, hauled up her shirt and studied her body. Was that what a pregnant woman looked like? Certainly her skin glowed—though that could be something to do with a succession of intensely satisfying orgasms.

She judged herself critically. The dark mass of her

rough-dried and tumbled hair looked undeniably sexy. There was a definitely sultry expression filling out her lips and making them look quite lush. No wonder Dan had grabbed her.

But was she pregnant? She sighed impatiently. She'd soon know one way or the other.

And feeling ravenously hungry, she went downstairs to cook up a huge pile of chips.

'Comfort food,' she mused, and tucked into a double helping of chocolate mousse. It could be the last wicked meal she ate for the next seven months.

She put down her spoon, suddenly unable to eat. The prospect of going through a pregnancy without Dan's support filled her with a terror that made her loins turn to water.

He'd always been there for her in the past. And she'd taken him for granted. Oh, sure, he was to blame for his roving libido. But she'd shut him out. Had been too tired for sex. What a mess she'd made of her life.

CHAPTER SIX

FOR the third day running, Dan cancelled all his appointments, sending his loyal secretary frantic.

'You can't afford the time, not now Celine's walked out,' Diane pointed out, looking harassed—as well she might. 'You have contracts set up, deals to clinch—'

'I know,' he agreed curtly. 'And I can't begin to think how I'll manage without her.' Heaving a heavy sigh, he said, 'I'm sorry to put you in this position but this is important to me, Diane. I must take this time off. I'll work a twenty-four-hour day for a while if necessary, to catch up. Give everyone my promise that the work will be done—'

'How about I call Celine at home and talk her round?' Diane suggested gently.

A spasm of pain tightened his mouth. The two hours with Celine had been a nightmare he didn't want to repeat.

'No,' he muttered. 'Our row touched the Richter scale and she went ballistic.'

Diane touched his hand in brief sympathy. 'I know what you thought of her, what your relationship meant. I'm sorry. If you need a shoulder, I'm here. In the meantime, I'll get on and ring your clients, then hold the fort till you return with the relief party.'

'Thanks. Appreciated.'

'You look awful. Will you be all right?' Diane asked tentatively.

'I've no idea,' he said, and left before he spilled his emotions on the office floor and compromised his self-control.

Preoccupied with keeping icily detached, he stalked into the cottage surgery and found Helen there alone, her face drawn and white and her cringing figure quite transparently indicating that she was a bag of nerves.

But he handled himself well, just giving her a curt nod and picking up a magazine, which might as well have been the Domesday Book for the attention he paid to it.

He slanted a quick glance at her and quite unexpectedly his body melted.

'It's not the Inquisition,' he murmured drily, aching to see how frightened she was.

'I wish it were,' she mumbled.

'I could set one up if you like,' he offered, hoping to amuse her.

She didn't look his way. Her heavy panic breathing made the fluid red sun-dress move seductively and he tightened his defences, focussing hard on an article about the menopause, absorbing enough of it to be amazed at what women went through.

'Not very popular, this doctor,' came Helen's tinny, scared voice.

He glanced around the empty room and felt worried. There wasn't even a receptionist. Had he brought Helen— the possible mother of his child—to some inadequate quack?

'Perhaps they're all healthy hereabouts,' he suggested, hiding his qualms.

If the doctor didn't come up to scratch, Dan vowed, he'd cut the interview short and whisk her off to a specialist. Didn't matter how much it cost. She had to have the best.

'Doesn't look like a waiting room,' she ventured, with a brave attempt at conversation.

Judging that she needed diverting, he put down the magazine and made an effort to entertain her.

'Must be the least clinical surgery I've ever been in,' he agreed. 'If all waiting rooms had comfortable armchairs and mustard sofas, I imagine they'd make patients feel a lot better. Can't think why it's not full of people discussing the constant rain, global warming and the rocketing price of umbrellas.'

'I suppose this is the doc's sitting room when everyone's gone home.'

The subdued Helen leaned forward and warmed her trembling hands by the log fire, which burned in the inglenook.

'Well, let's make ourselves at home, since we're clearly being invited to. That aroma of roasted coffee beans is irresistible.' Dan went over to the antique table beneath a lattice window where a tray was laid with refreshments. 'Coffee for you?' he asked politely, his hand on the percolator.

'Should I?' she asked, her grey eyes glistening with unshed tears.

How would he know? Suddenly he felt shocked by his ignorance about nutrition and dos and don'ts for pregnant women. Though he had to remember she might *not* be carrying his baby.

It felt as if a bucket had scooped out his insides and he knew that this baby was more important to him than he'd imagined.

Desperate to hide his emotional response from her, he turned back to the tray.

'You could try the fruit teas they've got here.' He examined them, taking solace in reading out the labels. 'Chamomile. Raspberry, ginger and lemon—'

'Chamomile. I think it's calming,' she said, sounding as if she needed a proper tranquilliser.

But drugs like that were taboo, of course. Even he knew that she had to watch what she ate.

If she was pregnant. The bucket did a good job of excavating his stomach again. In the absence of a stiff brandy, he'd settle for a shot of caffeine.

Unnerved by the store he was putting in this baby, he handed her the drink, steadying her hand when it shook so hard that the cup rattled noisily in the saucer.

She let his fingers remain for a while and he stupidly put himself on the rack, yearning to pull her into his arms, to nuzzle her gloriously silky hair, to kiss her trembling lips...

His imagination even allowed him to think that the atmosphere between them had thickened with desire. That she ached for him and was holding herself back with difficulty.

Fool. As she'd said, if there *were* any sparks still around, it was either his imagination, or her body living in the past. Mentally, she'd written him off.

With a quick gesture he withdrew his hand and left her cup to its fate. It was a while before his heart rate had settled down again and he'd got his stupid, desperate hunger locked up in its cage once more.

Sipping the rich, Arabian coffee appreciatively, he chafed at the wait. The less time he and Helen spent together, the better.

He searched for further diversion. 'Nice little cottage, isn't it? I imagine it's unique to find a doctor's surgery in a thatched house with hollyhocks and poppies and country flowers outside.'

God. He was babbling. But anything to stop his longing to sweep Helen up and to comfort her. All he could hear was the clattering of her cup. She was in an even worse way than he was.

'Coffee's good,' he remarked. 'Surprised he can afford such treats with so few patients—'

He whirled, alerted by the way Helen had slid her cup to the table and scrambled to her feet with a gasp.

'I can't go in!' she whispered hoarsely. 'I can't—'

'Mrs Shaw. Mr Shaw! Welcome!' beamed the grey-haired man who'd just emerged from an inner sanctum. 'I won't be a moment.'

Helen gulped while the doctor chatted cheerfully to his patient and they discussed a later appointment to fit around the Women's Institute meeting. To Dan's surprise, Helen's hand stole into his.

'Seems a nice guy,' he muttered encouragingly under his breath. Her grip increased its pressure. 'Feeling sick?' he asked huskily.

'No. Just petrified.' She flashed him a brave but wobbly smile. 'Worse than exams. Can I opt for the Inquisition now instead?'

'Too late,' he soothed. 'I think we're on.'

'Well! This is pleasant!' declared the smiley doctor, after a cheery wave to his patient. He closed the door and gave them his full attention. 'Let's see…you've taken Deep Dene, haven't you? Lovely house. You'll be very happy there once you've finished the building work. Come on in and make yourselves comfortable for our chat. I've got some chocolate biscuits in here somewhere…'

Dan raised an amused eyebrow at Helen behind the doctor's back and she managed an answering half-smile before it faded and she was back in trembling mode again.

His own heart was thudding like a steam hammer but he squared his shoulders, took a deep breath and bustled her in.

Let her be pregnant. Then he could salvage something good from this disaster. He'd learnt during his time with Helen that he had a secret well of love to offer someone. At least it could be diverted to his child—and then he wouldn't feel the crucifying need to squander his emotions on someone who didn't want him.

Gripping Helen's hand tightly for reassurance—his or hers?—he sat with her on a cream sofa, the doctor settling himself comfortably in an armchair opposite.

How often, Dan thought painfully, had his love been thrown back in his face? When would he ever learn? Still, he consoled himself, his child would be different. The only person he'd be able to trust. They'd build up a bond so strong that nothing could break it. This was his one hope for the future. His one chance of unconditional love.

Please. Be pregnant. Have my baby. He almost yelled it out. Contained himself with incredible difficulty. And prepared himself for the gut-wrenching disappointment just as a precaution.

'Well, Mrs Shaw,' said the doctor with an encouraging smile, offering the biscuits. 'Tell me what's bothering you.'

Helen took a biscuit and nibbled it absently. Dan had a crazy desire to lick the chocolate from her lips.

'I think I might be pregnant,' she said in a pitifully small voice.

Dr Taylor's eyes warmed with sympathy. 'I see. And would you say that's good or bad?' he asked in a kindly tone.

'Good!' Dan blurted out. 'We're desperate to know for sure, if everything's all right—the baby, Helen…!' He couldn't go on, his fears overcoming him.

'Mrs Shaw?' murmured the doctor, after nodding at Dan's contribution. 'You seem agitated.'

Dan noticed how shrewd the man's eyes were. He was making judgements, Dan thought. Seeing the doctor's gaze on his fiercely clenched hands, Dan placed them in an unconvincingly relaxed pose on his knees and waited anxiously for Helen's reply. The doctor wasn't fooled, Dan realised. He knew his body was shaking with tension.

'It's come as a surprise. We hadn't planned… But… I-I'd be terribly upset if I'm not,' Helen replied in a squeak.

Dan hauled in a harsh breath. Yes—and he'd be devastated. Sound roared in his ears as his mind dealt with that. Suddenly Helen's hand was tugged from his. The doctor was talking to her amiably, taking her to a screen in the corner of the room.

Incapable of keeping still, Dan tried to compose himself and to prepare more thoroughly for the possibility that their conclusion had been wrong. A pain sliced through his chest, making his body contract with pain.

But he had to face facts. If they *were* mistaken, he'd get far away. Canada, the States, Australia…any continent that didn't have Helen living on it.

Please, please let there be a child, he repeated like a mantra. Or where the hell would he channel the terrifying hunger for love that he'd kept so successfully hidden up to now?

Stunned—and with a million questions whirling in her head, Helen stumbled out of the cottage with Dan a whole hour later. During that time she had answered the most detailed and searching questions about herself and had found herself liking and respecting Dr Taylor more and more as he'd imparted information and revelations on how she might produce a healthy baby.

Pregnant. She was going to be a mother—*was* a mother.

She couldn't breathe. Stopped dead. A baby. Inside her.

'Just a minute,' she croaked as Dan, unaware of her bemused state, tugged her on.

'Sure,' he rasped, and leant against the porch, his hand loose around hers.

From the patient way he waited, she knew he'd realised what a monumental shift this would be in her life, and he was giving her time to adjust to the shock.

But Helen knew she had to get a grip. With deliberate care she focussed on her breathing, intent on returning it to normal instead of its hectic gasping.

In-two-three, out-two-three. In-two-three-four, out-two-three-four. And now she could smell the scent of the honeysuckle, which twined artfully around the old plank door. Another moment or two and she'd be fully back to normal again.

Normal? She bit her lip. She'd virtually have to become a different person. Being a mother meant putting your child before everything else. She was used to her independence, to coming and going when and where and how she liked, to the frantic stimulation of London and the non-stop activity of ringing phones, meetings, decision making…

How would she cope? Clutching Dan's hand tightly, she stood stock-still in the weak sunshine and gazed blankly ahead, hurtling towards a world in which she was an ignorant novice. After years of her being acclaimed as bright and steel-minded with sound financial judgement, this was a novelty she did not welcome.

I know nothing, she thought with increasing alarm. And she had no mother around to guide her, no one—other than the doctor—to steer her through the enormous task of caring for her baby. It petrified her.

'Would you know it? A rainbow,' mused Dan huskily, looking up at the great bow that bridged the horizon. 'Seems appropriate. Sign of hope for the future.'

Her mouth pinched in. It was all right for him. All he had to do was to turn up every other Saturday bearing presents and exuding *bonhomie*. A few coos over the pram and that would be it for another week.

She'd be lumbered with the sleepless nights and nappies and the fear that she might drop her baby and kill it...

Hastily Helen crushed the wild panic, searching for the good bits. Because she would have the best of it. For a start, she'd have her baby's trust. The feel of her child in her arms, someone to love... The tension in her body flowed away, to be replaced by a quiet joy. She *was* happy about the baby and would get the hang of motherhood as most women did.

That part of her life wasn't her main worry now. It was Dan. Already she missed his presence desperately. And it would get worse.

In his jeans and cream shirt he looked utterly edible. Trouble was, some other woman was currently tasting the delights of his flesh. Her face darkened. Celine must think she'd died and gone to heaven.

With painful gentleness, he turned her to him, his hands resting lightly on her arms. Her stomach flipped over with arousal.

'Poor Helen. It's been a shock, hasn't it? So totally unexpected, and to happen now...' He bit his lip as he stared down at her tragic face. 'Are you all right?' he asked, with quiet concern.

Longing to sink into his embrace, to feel the comfort of his strong arms around her, she remembered where he'd stayed the night—and what he'd probably been up to—and muttered morosely, 'No. I'm all jumbled up inside.'

He frowned. 'You are...*pleased*?'

For a moment he looked so vulnerable that her treacherous heart suddenly filled with love. Helpless to stop herself, she let her eyes close and she lifted her face to his.

Kiss me, her mouth said. Hold me. Be a father to our baby...

Feeling a movement, her eyes jerked open. His hand had come beneath her elbow, gripping tightly. She protested, feeling the pressure. And then went along with it, allowing him to virtually force her along the long garden path towards the open gate.

'There are things I want to say to you,' he announced curtly as she struggled to match his ground-swallowing strides. 'It's a long time since the weather was halfway decent so I suggest we walk for a bit and get things clear. Neutral ground. There's a lot to discuss.'

'Like what?'

He flung a glance back at her small, unhappy face and he stiffened, snatching away his cupped hand as if she were tainted.

'I would have thought that was obvious. Essentially, we need to break away from one another,' he explained coldly, pausing to let her through the gate.

Helen managed to mask her disappointment. She was used to having her hopes of a reconciliation dashed.

'I thought we had,' she responded tartly.

'We're still tied to one another,' Dan growled.

She came to an abrupt halt just outside the gate. He meant divorce. All the nasty details about selling up... Her heart thumped. She shuddered, and was about to move on when she suddenly noticed the doctor's brass plaque.

'That's odd. He's a medical doctor *and* a homoeopath,' she commented in surprise.

Dan grunted. 'I wondered why we weren't out in ten minutes flat. Sorry about that. I didn't notice. I'll get you registered with someone else—'

'No, it's all right,' she said firmly, a great calm settling on her. 'I liked him very much. I got the impression that my feelings mattered, which was a novelty. And I was interested in the options he gave me for childbirth.'

Her hand quite naturally closed over her abdomen as she mentally greeted her child and her voice lowered to a warm husk.

'I want this baby to be protected and safe,' she said, feeling she was in charge of her own body, managing the baby's environment. 'As far as possible, I'm going to avoid all pollutants, now and for ever. And I trust Dr Taylor enough to take the natural remedy he suggested for morning sickness. You know something? I feel better already, even after the one dose.'

'What about this nutrition stuff?' asked Dan doubtfully, waving the sheets in his hand.

'Fresh, organic food? No contaminants? Makes sense to me,' she replied, pleased with her new-found knowledge and eager to know more.

'Hmm. But you'll need proper drugs during the birth—'

'No. I'm willing to put my faith in Dr Taylor's treatments. Dan, he made perfect sense when he talked about using natural and safe remedies. I don't want the baby to start life with a mass of drugs in its body,' she declared, quite astonished and overwhelmed by the fierce, protective passion she felt for her unborn child.

Dan shrugged, clearly not convinced. 'Whatever you say. Only I warn you, I will intervene during the birth if I think the baby's at risk.'

Her eyes rounded. 'You…you mean to be there?' she squeaked.

'At the birth? Of course. I have a vested interest, remember?'

Helen bridled and set off down the village street, trying to deal with that. It was such a personal thing to do. And by then Dan would have been living with Celine for some months.

Sexy, luscious Celine. Helen let the jealousy surface. Some time during the third week in January, Dan would be torn from Celine's arms to watch his inflated, pregnant, ex-wife pant and scream her way through agonising hours, in the most undignified position imaginable. She'd seen films. She knew what it was like.

'You can wait outside and pace up and down. I don't want you there!' she stated with unusual ferocity.

'Why?' he countered.

Vanity. Humiliation. Because it would only remind her of what might have been, at a time when she'd be emotionally vulnerable. In an unguarded moment of sentimental slush she might even beg Dan to come back to her. And he'd look at her whale-shaped body with horror and crush her self-esteem for ever.

'You won't be my husband by then,' she said sullenly. 'I want my birth partner to be someone who's close to me.'

'Like who?' he shot through clenched teeth.

'How should I know? Perhaps my mother. Or I might have made friends with someone here, or fallen madly in love with some guy—'

He looked at her in shock. 'You're pregnant! You can't do that!'

Helen groaned inwardly. How had she got into this stupid discussion? Now she'd have to justify her position!

'You can't help your feelings,' she said sniffily. 'Love happens. I'm not a complete dog, Dan. It's quite possible I'll meet someone who thinks I'm fantastic, and I'm certainly not ruling it out just because I'm pregnant!'

Dan's eyes were cold and hard and his manner was menacing. 'I had no idea that it would be so easy for you to switch your affections,' he muttered. 'It says a lot about the superficiality of your so-called love for me.'

This was terrible. She was being backed into a corner, saying things she didn't really mean. She'd never love anyone as much as she'd loved Dan. And it annoyed her that he was making out she was in the wrong for imagining some future love in her life. He was the one who'd been unfaithful!

'I could say the same about you,' she complained crossly. 'Your affair with Celine isn't my idea of showing depth of commitment to marriage.'

'I didn't have an affair,' he said tightly.

She shrugged. 'Still in denial, I see. Well, admit it or not, it's finished between us and I'm being realistic. I mean to move on. To put the past behind me and look for happiness elsewhere.'

'Another man.'

'Yes.' Her head jerked up in defiance, sending her hair swirling. 'Eventually.'

'I see,' he bit.

She sensed his tension. Of course he wouldn't like that. Men were very proprietorial about their ex-wives—she knew that from the heart-to-hearts she'd had in the office with women. And men. Also, she reasoned, he'd hate the idea of their child having a step-father who'd have more influence than him.

'I know it's an awful situation,' she said, her voice softening with sympathy. 'But we can't pretend our lives will be the same.'

With all her heart she wished he hadn't taken that irrevocable step and responded to Celine's advances. If only he'd thought of the consequences.

'I'm aware of that. Give me a minute. I'm thinking,' he muttered, waving an impatient hand at her for silence.

She shrugged and left him to it. The very fact that they maintained a distance between them, instead of holding hands or wrapping friendly arms around one another, made her feel extraordinarily sad.

She was thirty, Dan four years older. For the past sixteen years they'd been friends, lovers, companions and soul mates. Now it was as if those years had never been.

It seemed particularly cruel that a twist of fate had split them apart at such a special moment in their lives.

But she must accept what had happened and make something of her life. She wasn't the first woman in this situation and wouldn't be the last.

The responsibility of a child was huge, but she'd shoulder it. Decisively she drew herself more upright and, because Dan made no attempt to talk, she began to take notice of her surroundings.

The thatched cottages which lined the quiet lane had been built from flint some two hundred or so years ago, and their small gardens were—like Dr Taylor's—a riot of colour and sound as bees hummed busily in the bright summer flowers, frantic to gather pollen before the rain came again.

Delicious scents filled the air, swallows stretched their scimitar wings in an increasingly blue sky and a warm peace seemed to enfold the entire community.

'Morning!'

Surprised, Helen and Dan hastily found smiles for the complete stranger who'd greeted them, and they offered in return a quick 'hello'.

They were in the heart of the village. Beyond the duck pond on the traditional village green, a short, squat Saxon church sat on a small rise and Helen felt its ancient serenity reach out to her, offering peace, sanctuary and permanence.

For centuries, through war and plague, local and national disasters, the church had been there, solid and reassuring. It must have witnessed thousands of christenings, weddings and funerals. Comforted by the small church's survival, she decided she would make it her church, and that her baby would be christened there. She would survive this, somehow.

'There's a bench over there,' Dan said quietly. 'Let's sit down and talk.'

'"In memory of Dot Taylor,"' she said, reading from the small plate attached to the back of the bench. '"So that others may enjoy the same pleasure she had in feeding the ducks and watching a small and perfect world go by."' She gave a faint smile. Would that be the doctor's mother? 'That's lovely, Dan,' she said softly.

But he seemed unmoved by the sentiments. Tight-jawed, he was checking the seat, brushing it with his hand before they sat down. And even the comic arrival of a gang of noisy mallard ducks didn't crack the scowl on his face.

Helen clung to the little glimpse of a happier future that she'd stumbled upon. There would be a contentment of sorts. She and her baby would walk here, buy odd items at the little shop-cum-post-office, feed the ducks, say hello to strangers.

It occurred to her that all this time she'd been hurtling blindly off to work, she hadn't appreciated the balm to her soul that lay on her doorstep. She leaned back, soothed by the village atmosphere, by the lifestyle she'd share with her child.

'This baby is very important to me.' Dan's curt words broke in on her reverie.

Tense suddenly, she slanted a glance at his rigid profile, unable to make out his mood or his intention. Fear clutched at her. Was he going to fight her for custody?

'And to me!' she breathed, her pulses jerking about all over the place.

'You know the kind of childhood I had.'

Too well. Her heart softened and ached for him. 'Yes, Dan. I do.'

'You'll understand, then,' he said, eyes dark and burning upon her, 'why I don't want our child to suffer because of us.'

Helen blinked. What was he getting at? 'He, she, won't,' she said hastily. 'We might feel angry and bitter at the moment, but things will calm down and by the time the baby's born I'm sure we'll have formed a vaguely amicable relationship—'

'I don't want that.'

Her antennae quivered. 'You want us to be at war with one another?'

Dan looked away and stared unseeingly at the quacking ducks. It was obvious that he was very unhappy. Rips appeared in her heart again. He was so near, and yet so far, his familiar, muscular arms close enough to touch in a sympathetic and understanding gesture... But the gulf that yawned between them was unbridgeable.

'I want our child to have two parents,' he said flatly.

Puzzled, she replied, 'Of course it will!'

'No,' he said with deliberate care. 'I mean two biological parents who share in every part of our child's life.'

Helen gasped. 'You and me? You know that's impossible!'

Sculptured lips tightened in an obstinate line. 'There is a way.' He turned, fire and urgency setting his eyes alight. 'There must be. I can accept nothing less.'

'Dan—' she began uncertainly.

'Do I have to spell it out to you?' he demanded hotly. 'My hell won't be my baby's hell. It's as simple as that.'

He could hardly bear this. His mouth twisted with painful memories. Helen had made him resurrect things he'd buried long ago.

The life-long absence of his father, who'd pushed off when his mother had declared she was pregnant. A father he'd never known and didn't ever want to. But he'd longed for the love of a father, dear God, he wished he'd had that.

Other things crowded his mind, arousing emotions he'd carefully stifled. As a silent, indrawn child, he'd watched his mother grow thin and grey and old, while she'd worked from morning to night trying to scrape together enough money to feed them.

Sometimes at night he would wake to the sound of her heart-rending sobs and knew there was nothing he could do except be good, wash up, make the supper, keep out of her way, and do well at school so that he could look after her one day and care for her as he longed to.

His abiding memory was of wanting her attention, a hug, thanks for doing the chores, praise for the exams he passed. But he'd held back from telling her this because he'd known she'd been a walking automaton with no emotion to spare for him.

Each day he'd wondered who would be looking after him when the school day finished. He'd felt like a human pass the parcel: unwanted, unloved, a nuisance under sufferance.

Stay in the corner. Go to your room. Keep your mouth shut. Come near me and I'll belt you. His stomach churned. A hell of a life.

And then he'd met Helen.

He realised she was speaking.

'...except it's not the same situation, as yours was, Dan,' she was saying gently. 'I won't be penniless like your mother. I have good earnings, something put by. You are financially secure, too—'

'You don't understand!' he cried, passionate in his frustration. 'You never will because you didn't experience it! I wanted a father. I wanted a mother, not a string of childminders who stuck me in a corner. I wanted love. Someone to care. The money's *unimportant*. It's the emotional security that matters, Helen!'

'I can give that,' she retorted stubborn-mouthed.

'As far as I'm concerned, it won't be enough for my child!' he argued grimly. 'I've been there, remember. So listen. Try to understand. When my mother died and I was pushed from one set of foster parents to another, my dreams were filled with images of what I imagined other children had: a mother and father, listening to the events of their day, helping them with homework, caring, loving, arguing maybe... I know it's probably nothing like reality, that thousands of children grow up happy and healthy with only one parent. But not for my child. I couldn't allow that. Helen,' he said, his voice cracking, 'the last thing in the world I ever wanted was for a child of mine to go through life without proper parents—'

'It won't!' she protested. 'I keep saying, you'll be there. You can have access any time you like—'

'That's not what I want.'

Her breath became laboured. Wide-eyed with apprehension, she said warily, 'What are you suggesting, Dan?'

He sucked in a breath and let it out, hard and sharp.

'Let's start from the beginning. You said you wanted to avoid pollution and stress, to bring our child up as healthily as possible.'

She licked her lips. Now what?

'Yes. I do.'

'Then Deep Dene is an ideal place for that.'

Relief made the breath exhale sharply from her lungs, too. They'd find a way to keep her there! A small, wry smile touched the corners of her lips.

'I couldn't agree more,' she said fervently. 'And I've got a confession to make. A short while ago I would have said that Deep Dene was the last place I wanted to live. Up to a short time ago, I hated it, Dan. I'm sorry,' she said. 'I tried to love it because you did. Now I *do* love it—because it is everything I want for our child.' She smiled softly to herself, thinking of her baby sheltering within her body, and the lovely environment it would one day enjoy. 'I love this village, too. The downs, the whole way of life... I don't know how I'll juggle that and working, but—'

'That's the point I'm coming to,' he said, the quietness of his voice belying the passion in his eyes. 'I certainly want you to live in Deep Dene because I want our child to grow up there. It's everything I ever wanted.'

'You'll find it hard to leave,' she said hesitantly.

His mouth tightened. 'I would—if I did leave,' he said cryptically. 'Helen, I want a closer bond with our baby than you're anticipating—and what I'm suggesting will mean you won't have to find a babysitter or a nanny or a crèche. You see, I don't want to be a visitor to my own child. That isn't the same as experiencing closely the bedtime routines, daily problems, and the milestones in a child's life.'

She stared. The penny slowly dropped. He could only mean one thing. That he wanted to heal the rift between them, to start afresh and for their family to be whole.

Much as she wanted that, she wasn't sure it would work. He'd cheated on her. Maybe he would again. The risk was enormous.

But perhaps he was truly sorry. She bit her lip, trying not to be swayed by her reckless heart, which was urging her to agree and leap into his arms with forgiving kisses on her lips.

'I'm not sure,' she said slowly.

'I want this more than anything,' he husked.

She felt herself sway under the influence of his molten tar gaze and she had difficulty in keeping her mind on track.

If she rejected his apology now, they'd remain enemies for ever because he'd never forgive her for being such a cow. Yes, or no. His future, hers, the baby's, lay entirely in her hands.

CHAPTER SEVEN

HELEN'S heart had no problem with forgiveness, her head said 'maybe'. It went without saying that her body had long ago surrendered. In confusion, she concentrated on what would be best for the baby and came up with the answer: stability and constant love.

That posed a problem. What if Dan strayed and deserted her and her child? If he was doing this for all the wrong reasons—to keep control of the baby—then staying together would never work and he'd leave eventually. But how would she ever be sure what had prompted his request?

'Don't deny me this out of spite.'

Startled by Dan's low growl, she glanced up at him. When her eyes locked with his, she was shaken by the waves of tight passion that crackled and leapt across the space between them.

He wanted this desperately. If only she knew why.

'Supposing you hang around and then...then you change your mind?' she ventured.

'How can you suggest that? I wouldn't. I'd be totally committed.' He coughed, clearing a surprisingly gravelly throat. And studied the duck pond with unusual interest. But she saw that his jaw was set in determination, the sculpting of his mouth firm and decisive. 'I would be constant. Reliable.' The tip of his tongue moistened his lips. 'You must know how I feel,' he added softly.

A smile found its way to her lips. Hazily she realised he was in as much turmoil as she. Dan was so worried that she'd turn him down, that he dared not even look at her.

Affectionately she hugged his reticence to herself. And hid her own ecstasy for the time being.

'Yes. I think I do,' she murmured demurely, finding it hard to remain calm when her entire body fizzed and bubbled with delight. He would apologise for his behaviour, and she would forgive him. She tried not to grin happily. 'I think you're right. You should be part of our child's life. A big part.'

'Fine.'

On pins, she waited for him to take her in his arms and beg her forgiveness. And then they'd be able to make up.

Abruptly he stood up and began to prowl up and down in front of her like a feral animal, dark, lithe and loose-limbed, scattering ducks and impecunious sparrow hangers-on in the process. He was finding this difficult, she thought in fond amusement.

But of course she wouldn't hesitate to have him back if he was truly contrite. It would take a while for trust to re-establish itself, but it would be worth making the effort. They had a child to consider.

Happily she stroked her stomach, watching Dan's brooding face and waiting for his closed expression and the tension of his body to ease up as he broached the idea of their reconciliation.

She loved him so much. More than she'd ever known before all this had blown up. Life without him was unthinkable. She had come through the bitterness and hatred and could now let go of her negative feelings. There was only one man for her. Dan. The father of her child. Love poured into her, emptying itself into her aching heart and easing all her pain. Deliriously happy, she smiled.

In her mind she saw them cooing idiotically over their newborn baby. Dan, pushing the pram with a huge beam of pride splitting his face. Dan snuggled up to her while she fed their baby...

'I propose this,' he said, still heart-wrenchingly stilted. 'I want us to stay married.'

Her eyes closed in brief thanks. Everything would be all right! And how funny he was, telling her in a round-about way that he really did love her! Helen did her best to be encouraging and yet appear innocent of his intentions. He needed to feel that he was making all the running. This was part of his act of contrition.

'I think that's a good idea, too,' she said levelly.

He grunted and elaborated on his plan. 'Good. You stop work as soon as you can—'

'But I don't—!'

'Do you want to commute, to be assailed by petrol fumes and the stress of a twelve-hour day? To risk losing the baby?' he demanded, looking at her askance.

Put like that... 'No. Of course I don't, but other women work and—'

'You are not other women. Your job is draining. You know that.'

'Yes,' she said doubtfully, the idea appealing to her more and more. She could opt out of the rat race for a while, spend time relaxing and walking, making a home— a real home—at Deep Dene. 'But financially—'

'No problem.' He was the old Dan now, full of confidence and strength of will. 'Business is booming and I can provide you with a good income so you're effectively independent.'

'It seems a bit one-sided,' she demurred. But she felt cherished. Protected. It was lovely.

'No. You will be bringing up our child,' he replied. 'That's more important than anything. My intention is to live in London till the baby's born so I can concentrate on work, but naturally I will check every day that you're

OK. That'll keep us apart for a while, which—I'm sure you'll agree—will suit us both very well.'

This wasn't going right. Helen's brow furrowed. He seemed to be heading for a different solution from the one she'd imagined.

'Go on,' she said warily, her spine suddenly chilled.

'When the baby's born, naturally I will return to live in Deep Dene.' Dan paused in his relentless pacing and stared at the ground as if it had done him an injury. 'By that time, the builders will have gone—and I'll have turned the study, the library and the downstairs bathroom into a small flat for myself. I could also turn the dairy into a kitchen and take the whole west side for my garden. We'd hardly see one another from one day to the next.'

She was speechless. Her mouth gaped.

Dan's guarded glance made her cringe. It was bleak and impersonal. Her head whirled. She'd made a terrible mistake.

'We both own the house,' he stated, for all the world like an accountant discussing a balance sheet. 'I have as much right to live in it as you.'

'A...*flat*?' she repeated stupidly.

'Place is big enough,' he replied crisply, still in accountant mode.

Absently he picked a wild daisy and began systematically to remove its petals. She watched, appalled, checking off each petal with 'he loves me, he loves me not, he loves me...' And of course it ended with 'he loves me not'. What else?

'It is,' she breathed, playing for time.

'Makes sense, doesn't it?'

With an impatient movement he threw the bare stem away and the ducks came running to see if it was good to eat. They were as disappointed as she was, she thought glumly. He loved her not.

What an idiot she was. Self-torture in one easy lesson by Helen Shaw. Expert in her field.

'You—you said you'd be constant, reliable...'

'That goes without saying. I won't ever desert the baby. I will always be part of our child's life.'

'Oh!' Now she understood. He'd not been thinking of her at all. She felt herself shrink. 'How would this arrangement work in practice?' she managed to croak.

'Simple. When the baby's born I will go out to meet clients and assess their needs as usual, but increase the amount of work I do from home. We can organise a routine so that certain days or times are mine and you can take a break. Go off and have your hair done. Go shopping, take a part-time job, whatever. I can then be properly involved in my child's life. We can do it, Helen. For our child's sake, we must be civilised and adult about this. Speak politely to one another. Be friends, as far as we can. There must be no bad atmosphere, no recriminations, no bitterness. Our child must feel safe and secure and loved by both of us.'

He couldn't be serious. Struggling with Dan's suggestion, she stared at him in appalled dismay as her hopes finally crashed about her ears. Again. She groaned. Why did she keep putting herself through this? Though she knew the answer. Because she loved him.

'You...want us to live in the same house—but separately—and to act as if we're two child-minders who take turns to look after our baby?'

His head jerked around and she cringed at the pain searing his dark eyes. 'Not child-minders. *Parents!* I want to know my child!' he rasped. 'I want my child to know me and not to see me as a Saturday father! I want real knowing. To be there for him or her when there are problems. To be confided in. To be loved, truly loved.'

Her heart lurched. Despite her own misery, she recognised that this was his baby, too, and men—even *loving* husbands—had the short straw where child-care was concerned. They could never know what it was like to nurture a baby inside you, or the miracle of giving birth—however uncomfortable or painful either of those situations might be.

Already she felt at one with her baby. She could talk to it, include it in her daily life. Dan was just an onlooker.

She pressed a hand to her swollen breast and thought of the time when her son or daughter would be in her arms. Still dreaming, she lifted lazy lashes to meet Dan's gaze. And quivered at what she saw.

Naked hunger. Drowsy sensuality.

'Dan?' she queried uncertainly.

'Don't look at me like that!' he muttered.

He wants me, she thought in amazement. No. More than that. He needs me. Or…was she mistaken again?

Small pinpricks of excitement sent her skin tingling. Her eyes had ostensibly lowered, but she'd checked his body and there was no mistaking the newly taut stretch of his denim jeans.

Her optimism recovered itself. Maybe everything was not lost. Her original idea that they could come back together again wasn't so stupid after all. They had too much of a history between them, too many memories of happier times.

And she had something infinitely more precious than Celine possessed. She was carrying Dan's child.

A brief doubt slipped into her mind and she zapped it. He did want her. It was a start—something to build on. Petrified she might be, but she had to stick her neck out. An inch at a time. *Caution*, she warned herself. No playing easy to get or he'd run a mile.

They'd take things slowly and in time, because he'd said it was important, she would overcome her terrible jealousy and the thought of Celine in his arms would become a nasty memory, nothing more.

They would become friends, then lovers again—especially as they'd be living in the same house, making arrangements together, liaising, oh, yes, she could see it all!

A request to change a plug, mend the washing machine...a smile, a touch, growing desire... Plenty of floaty, cleavage-revealing clothes, the odd invitation to a shared meal, a tap on his door for borrowed sugar...

Her heart raced. They'd get back together, she was sure. And when he felt secure, she'd persuade him that he could safely admit to adultery and be forgiven.

Then there was the baby. With the joy of their newborn child softening his heart, he'd forget Celine's ample charms and realise what he could lose: the family he'd always longed for.

Her decision showed the triumph of hope over experience, she thought wryly. And amended that. Love conquered all. It would, she vowed. She would make certain of that! The Celines of this world would not win. Why should they?

Celine had broken them up—but only because something had been missing in their marriage. Helen vowed that she would put the shattered scraps of their love back together again and create the life she and Dan had always yearned for.

Intensely happy, she let her mouth curve into a delicious smile and she ventured a half-flirty, half-enquiring look at him.

Yes! That was enough to make him go weak at the knees. He was in *pieces*! Baffled, confused, longing for the love they'd once shared...yes. He was needy. Yes, she could do it. Must, for their baby's sake, for her own happiness.

Dan wanted his baby's love. He also wanted adult love. And she was going to be the one who provided that.

Recklessly risking all, she took a deep breath and sealed her fate.

'I think it's a very sensible idea,' she commented, anxious to sound reasonable and neutrally polite. 'You arrange it, Dan. I'll hand in my notice. Once I've found a replacement, I'll leave.' She thought a gesture was in order and stood up. 'I want us to remain friends for our child's sake. We can be adult about this. I promise I'll do my best to make this...relationship work.'

And as she kissed first one hot cheek and then the other she felt the tremor that ran through him and it was all she could do not to surrender herself then and there.

I'd walk through fire for him, she thought fiercely as they walked back to the car without speaking further. If I have to live without him for the next six months, then I will—if it means that we'll be together for the rest of our lives.

Her strides became liquid and flowing, her body swinging with the sense of freedom and joy that surged like a bird in her heart.

And beside her, she was gleefully aware that Dan was finding it increasingly hard not to grab her and kiss her breathless. He's mine! she exulted. In time, life was going to be wonderful. Just *perfect*. All she needed was patience.

The days slipped by. Dan remained in digs in London and one evening when she came home, it was to find that every item of his clothing had gone.

It gave her a shock. All trace of him had been removed and the bathroom didn't seem the same, particularly without the ridiculous teddy-bear-shaped flannel she'd given him as a joke.

But this was only temporary, she reminded herself. His

gear would be cluttering up the place by late January, when the baby was born. And he'd be back in her bed.

In two weeks she had found her replacement and left work. Time rolled on more slowly because, apart from the builders, she was alone all day at Deep Dene. If she hadn't been so determined to win Dan back she might have succumbed to doubts, but she didn't allow herself to weaken.

The grit that had driven her from schoolgirl to high-paid executive stood her in good stead. She had set her heart on a reconciliation and that was what she expected. Nothing less.

Her dreams were filled with him. Although she had grown to love Deep Dene, had mastered the Aga and now ignored the spiders, she missed Dan dreadfully and waited eagerly for his twice-daily phone calls, hearing the tiredness in his voice…and to her joy, the warmth, too.

'Helen? It's me.'

'Hello, me,' she murmured, with the maximum of seduction lurking in her voice.

There was a very satisfying frog in Dan's throat when he asked, 'How are you?'

Wilting, she thought contentedly, curling up on the sofa for a long and satisfying chat. Melting from top to toe. Gorgeous.

'Fabulous,' she cooed, sounding like a husky smoker on sixty a day.

'You don't miss…' he paused and she held her breath '…work?'

She smiled, sure in her own mind that he'd been intending to ask if she missed *him*.

'Oddly enough, no,' she said warmly. 'I feel a bit as if I've been released from prison. I can concentrate solely on the baby and the house and I'm reading mother and baby books like you'd never believe.'

'And there's the in-house entertainment as well. I suppose you're still dealing with the builders and their love lives,' he said in amusement, referring to an earlier conversation.

Helen laughed. 'Oh, yes. We're having great heart-to-hearts. They lean against the Aga rail and I fuss about, making yet another pot of tea for them. They get so many cuppas and go through so many packets of chocolate biscuits that they feel honour-bound to work hard in between!' she said with a giggle. 'And they're very sweet. I still can't do a thing in the garden without one of them rushing out to tick me off and grab a fork from my hot little hand!'

'I'm not surprised. You could charm for England,' Dan said, laughter in his voice. 'And I told them to keep an eye on you.'

'Did you, Dan?' she asked, touched.

'Don't want you overdoing things and harming the baby,' he replied gruffly. 'Now. Are you still eating properly? No rushed snacks?'

He cares, she thought blissfully. 'The fridge and larder are full of organic fruit and veg and I'm packed to the eyeballs with vitamins and nourishment,' she assured him solemnly. 'I feel healthier than I can remember.' Stronger, too, she thought. Clear-eyed, clear-headed and absolutely rock-solid sure about Dan. 'What about you?' she asked with affection threading through her words. 'I suppose you're existing on plastic sandwiches and sawdust as usual?'

He grunted. 'Never mind me. What about this scan thing tomorrow?'

'Ultrasound,' she informed him happily. 'It's so exciting, Dan! I'll see the baby and get printouts of the picture! I can't wait.' She hesitated, her voice wistful as she added, 'I suppose you can't get down to be with me for the photo shoot?'

She kept her fingers crossed. It would be a wonderful, bonding moment.

'No. I'm in York and travelling north. Can't make it,' he answered crisply. 'Keep a copy for me. Must go. Speak to you tomorrow. Bye.'

He rang off before she could properly say goodbye, too. But although she was disappointed, she knew why he was breaking his neck trying to get as much work done as possible. By the time the baby arrived his company would be well and truly on its feet and he'd be able to take time off to be with her.

She grinned. And *then* watch out, Dan Shaw! You won't know what's hit you!

Tomorrow she would see her baby. And maybe when Dan saw the ultrasound photo his heart would be touched and he'd declare his love in an outburst of passion.

Helen stretched luxuriously, her eyes softening as she imagined herself flying into his arms and all the anger and hurt melting away with their loving kisses.

'Soon, my little duck,' she promised her baby, 'you might have your father back.'

And she went up to bed certain that something was about to change her life for ever.

The hospital was half an hour away. Arriving late—because she'd been told there was always a two hour wait whatever time you turned up—she sailed blithely into the busy clinic, drank the required amount of water straight off and sat down beside a harassed looking mother who was trying to juggle three tiny children as well as her 'bump'.

Crikey! she thought sympathetically and caught a toddler as it flung itself recklessly over her outstretched foot. And then and there she revised her plans to have four children. Two would be fine.

'Thanks,' sighed the mother in a flat, dispirited tone.

'It's OK. My, you've got your hands full,' she ventured, alarmed by the woman's grey complexion.

Helen was uncomfortably aware how bright and fresh she must look in her daffodil-yellow sun-dress and matching pumps and felt almost apologetic about her rude health.

The woman gave her a jaundiced look. 'First time?' she enquired, batting one child with the back of her hand and attempting to catch a drippy nose with the other.

'Er…yes.'

'Thought so. You'll learn. Wait till you get projectile vomiting,' she warned darkly.

Heavens! Sounded awful! Helen thought, jumping up in agitation when she heard her name being called. Following the nurse, she looked around and was alarmed to see that most of the women looked depressed and resigned while children of varying ages hurtled around yelling their heads off.

This wasn't what she'd imagined at all. Her legs felt weak and wobbly.

'Sanctuary,' the nurse said wryly as the door of the examination room closed behind them.

'Is it always like that?' Helen probed.

'No. Sometimes it's worse,' conceded the nurse. 'OK. Let's be having you. On your own?'

Helen nodded. 'My husband's in York,' she said wistfully.

'Lucky him.'

Helen was startled by the nurse's cynicism. The edge had been taken from her pleasure. Nevertheless, she lay on the couch and comforted herself with the knowledge that she would soon be looking at her baby. Even the curt, rushed-off-his-feet doctor didn't dent her determined enthusiasm.

Until the picture on the screen became clear.

She froze. People were talking to her but she hardly heard. With startled eyes rounded in horror, she nodded as if she understood just so they'd stop and leave her alone. Someone hauled her off the couch, handed her the photo printouts and told her to get dressed.

With shaking hands she did so, fumbling with her buttons like a drunk. She had to get home. Ring Dan.

Oh, God! she moaned, running out of the cubicle, a sea of surprised faces turning in her direction as she flew through the clinic and blindly thrust open the outer door. Numb with shock, she waited at the bus stop outside.

What was she to do? She wanted Dan. Wanted him *now*. Oh, so very, very badly!

Dan had never driven dangerously in his life. But this time, his head reeling from the sound of Helen's hysterically pleading cries, he had come close to breaking the law. Only the knowledge that he wasn't one hundred per cent in control of his body, that it shook with agitation and foreboding and sheer panic, forced him to keep to the speed limit. Just.

It had taken him hours of non-stop driving to reach Deep Dene and now it was dark. He knew she'd been for a scan that day. It didn't take a genius to work out that she had learnt something terrible.

The baby. Dear heaven, the baby! He dragged his teeth hard across his lip. She'd been incoherent.

'Get here, Dan!' she'd screamed. 'Just get here!' she'd repeated, over and over again, not listening to his attempts to soothe her, unaware that he was going crazy with fear for her safety and that of the tiny life within her.

Shaking with tension, he had tried to reach Dr Taylor but had failed, picking up only the answering machine. Sick to the stomach, and fighting the urge to scream with frustration, he'd called Diane and had yelled at her to cancel everything till further notice and had then raced for his car as if the hounds of hell had been after him.

Now he was almost home and the nausea was churning up his guts, vying with his violent headache for his attention. But he could only think of Helen. And the baby.

Blanking out what might be wrong.

With scant regard for his car's suspension, he drove furiously up the lane and across the still-lumpy clay to the front door, stopping with a screech of brakes and a shudder of the outraged suspension.

'*Helen!*' he yelled, sending the front door flying.

Silence. His heart bounded like a hard cricket ball. He tried the drawing room first and there she was. Her mute, tear-stained face brought him to a shocked halt. He watched her stand up and prepare to speak and something about her abject misery kept him totally paralysed.

'You brute! How could you do this to me?' she whimpered pathetically.

He frowned, his breath still suspended in his chest. That wasn't what he'd been expecting.

'*What?*'

'*This!*'

On the edge of hysteria, she thrust something at him with an awkward jerk of her arm. Bewildered, he strode forwards and took the paper she held out, with so much fury in the simple gesture. It was a black and white printout, presumably the ultrasound image of their baby...

His jaw dropped. Every cell in his body froze as his brain dealt with the image before him.

Not a baby. *Two babies.*

CHAPTER EIGHT

DAN stared in disbelief at the picture of the two small faces, which were so perfectly outlined in profile against a dark background. Two up-tilted noses. A delicate chin each. The small curve of the skull. Skinny bodies lost in a swirl of white.

Twins. Two to love. Two to hold, to watch as they grew and learnt to toddle...

A huge rush of emotion swamped him. He wanted to cry. Did his best not to. These were his unborn children. It was nothing short of a miracle.

'Oh my good grief!' he breathed and floundered towards a seat and collapsed limply into it, overwhelmed by the bounty that had come into his life.

'I don't believe it!' he muttered, studying the strip again, mesmerised by the sight of the two perfect heads— when he'd expected a vague shape not remotely human. These were miraculously real with their detailed features. And he was looking at them. His children, his babies. The wonders of science, the wonder of nature. *'Helen!'* he murmured shakily, lifting his limpid gaze to her in awe.

She had already dropped down into the sofa again. His eyes were bleary with ecstatic tears but, when he impatiently brushed them with the back of his hand, he suddenly became aware of how incredibly beautiful she looked.

Her hair had grown since he'd last been here with her, and it fell in soft, shiny waves about her face. Despite her pallor there was a warm, rich peachiness to her skin, and a clarity to her stunningly smoky eyes that he remembered from her teenage days when her beauty and loving heart had knocked him for six.

The mother of his babies, he thought with a flash of sentimentality. His throat clogged up.

'I'm stunned. Words fail me,' he admitted, ruffling his hair in bewilderment.

'Well, they don't fail me! How *dare* you give me twins?' she jerked.

Affectionately he grinned, close to getting up and shouting for joy then running to the village and banging on everyone's door so they all knew, too.

'But it's wonderful, Helen!' he declared hoarsely, a stupid smile sitting blissfully on his face as if it would never, ever depart.

'You don't know anything!' she accused with a sniff. 'One baby's hard enough to manage, but *two*! You might have warned me if you had twins in your fam…' She went pink and bit her lip. 'I'm sorry,' she mumbled. 'I forgot you wouldn't know.'

Almost driven to take her in his arms and kiss her breathless, he got up and poured himself a drink instead, his hand quivering like a dipsomaniac's. Babies. Two of them, he kept thinking over and over in his mind. I'm a dad. Of twins!

'It's OK.' Bemused, he sipped the whisky, his heart skipping about like a kid in the playground. 'Am I relieved! You don't know what you put me through for the past few hours!' he declared ruefully. 'I thought you were seriously ill, or the baby was not normal in some way… I can't tell you what a nightmare the journey's been—'

'Really?' she quavered, her lower lip wobbling. But there was something bright and hopeful about her eyes.

Dan averted his gaze. 'Thought my kid was in trouble,' he said gruffly.

'Oh. Of course.' Her face fell. 'I'm sorry,' she said,

compressing her lips. 'I couldn't speak properly to explain. I just freaked out. My brain went into free fall.'

'I'm not surprised,' he said gently. 'I should have been there with you. I wish I had. I could have taken care of you.'

'That would have been nice.'

'How the devil did you get home in that state? You shouldn't have been driving—'

'I wasn't. I took the bus. It's a pretty journey.' She made a wry face. 'Well, it was nice on the way out. It could have been war-torn Beirut on the way back for all I knew.'

'Yes. I'm sure. What a shock you must have had,' he soothed and rubbed his moist eyes again.

'You look shattered,' she said sympathetically. 'Your eyes must be tired from concentrating on the road for so many hours. Thank you for coming. I'm sorry to have dragged you all this way but...I thought you should know.'

His eyes kindled because his head was full of dreams and bursting with love for his two—*two!*—babies. It was wonderful. Heart-stopping.

And...what else contributed to that surge of pleasure and affection? Did he detect a weakening of his resolve to be detached from her? It wasn't surprising. She looked so vulnerable. So utterly gorgeous in the bright yellow dress with its scooped neck that showed off her lovely throat. Dangerous, he warned himself. Not to be followed up in any way. But how he regretted not being with her during the scan...

'I really wish I'd gone with you today,' he told her with deep sincerity.

A movement in her throat told him that she had swallowed nervously. She managed a pathetic little laugh that touched his heart.

'Me, too. You could have stopped me from hyperventilating and running around like a headless chicken. I couldn't say much when they told me because I was at the hospital and they were madly busy—it was a bit of a production line, to be honest. The doctor hardly blinked when he saw the two heads. At first I thought...' she gulped, her voice wavering '...I thought it was *one* baby, d-de-f-*formed*!' she stumbled, bursting into tears.

'Oh, Helen!'

Desperately regretting his decision to stay in York—and thus avoid becoming emotional on seeing the first real evidence of their baby on the ultrasound monitor—he went over and sat next to her on the sofa. With a little sob that jerked from her trembling lips she came into his arms and he held her as close as he dared.

No kisses, he told himself. This is an old friend who's upset. Sympathy, comfort and understanding. But keep off the emotion stuff.

'I'm going to get the size of a marquee!' she said mournfully, unfortunately for him, raising her tear-streaked face to blink with heart-wrenching appeal. 'I'll never get my figure back!'

Dan stroked her arm reassuringly, fiercely trying to stick to his resolutions.

'Yes, you will. If necessary we'll hire a personal trainer to get you into shape afterwards. Though I doubt you'll need it,' he added with a rueful smile. 'You'll be pretty active, I should imagine.'

'I know!' She gave a horrified groan. 'Two babies at once! It's a nightmare! I'll never have time to go to bed! And...they said...they said I might have to have a Caesarean, Dan, and I don't *want* one, I want everything to be natural and soothing with lovely music and subdued lights and gorgeous scented oils burning in my aroma-therapy thing. I've planned it all!' she wailed. 'Instead I'll probably be bunged full of drugs to bring on the birth at a time suitable to the hospital, because they need a specialist on hand for twins—and I won't even be *conscious*!'

Flinging herself against him in a storm of weeping, she clung to him tightly while her body heaved up and down alarmingly.

'I want to see my baby—babies—born!' she sobbed. 'It's the best moment. Everyone cries buckets. But I'll go to sleep and when I wake up they'll be there—as if they're nothing to do with me!'

'Please, Helen,' Dan said anxiously. 'This isn't good for the babies.'

He began to worry as reality kicked in. It would be unbelievably tough on her. She'd need a lot of support. More than he'd been prepared to give. Now what?

'It's not good for me, either!' she wailed into his chest, which was feeling decidedly damp. 'For months I'll be b-blundering about like a—a hip-hippopotamus, knocking over chairs and sweeping entire meals off tables and waddling down the street in elasticated stockings and a h-horrible double-J-cup bra!'

Dan hid his smile in her hair. He loved her exaggerations. Adored and envied the way she leapt at life, emotions flying here, there and everywhere. He had never let go. Would never dare.

'It won't be that bad, Helen.'

'It will!' she yelled, deafening him. 'What do you know? You're a *man*!'

'Short of a sex change,' he said drily, 'I can't do anything about that. But I can be here with you from now on,' he offered, before he could stop himself.

She froze. 'What?'

And then she looked up with such a pathetic, unhappy face that he found himself saying, 'I mean it, Helen.'

'How?'

He thought rapidly. 'Easy,' he said, and invented a way,

off the top of his head. 'I can take on someone high-powered enough to do a good deal of my client work.' Who could do it? he wondered. Who'd have the skills, the sharpness of mind, the instant grasp of his business that would be needed? Ignoring the problem, he continued, in-venting an atmosphere of calm organisation. 'I can arrange things so I do *all* the programming here, at Deep Dene. I'll be in my study whenever you need a hand with some-thing and I can muck in every day. I helped get you in this, Helen. I think I ought to be here with you, whenever you need me.'

Her tears dried as if by magic. Shining-eyed, she stared at him with such naked trust that it made his heart turn over.

'You—you mean you're coming back to live here…*now*?' she breathed.

Someone help me! Dan thought in dazed confusion, his eyes fixed on her hypnotic lips. When would his sex urge die down?

'Uh-huh.'

'Oh, Dan!' she sighed, her sweet breath sending the sensors on his mouth into seizures. She seemed to wriggle and stretch with pleasure. Whatever it was, it had a star-tling effect on his hungry body. She let out a little sigh. 'Mmm. It would be lovely. Just marvellous!'

What would any red-blooded male do under those cir-cumstances? he found himself musing, two minutes into a long, breathless kiss. Helen had wound her arms around his neck and he couldn't escape, not without peeling her fingers off one by one.

Nor did he want to. It was glorious feeling her softness again. Letting the dammed-up passion flow out of his body. Settling down for a long and thorough exploration of her mouth. And neck. And throat.

He quivered. Firm, ripe breasts.

He was hot. Shed clothes. Felt her naked skin against his. How had that happened? Warmth enfolded him. His brain didn't exist.

This was the need for love. For the touch of a woman. A moment when he could pretend that all was well and they cared about each other. So what, if it was a lie? He couldn't stop. Didn't want to. And she wouldn't let him.

'Is it...?'

'Yes. It's all right. I've read the books,' she whispered.

Who was he to argue? Guided by her, he found himself on his back, watching hazily while she moaned above him in pleasure. His eyes closed as a tenderness cut through him like a knife. The gentleness, the sweetness of their love-making, pained and thrilled him.

Clenching his fists, he abandoned himself to his climax. But when she curled up beside him, murmuring contented little sighs, he went cold.

What had he done?

Her breathing slowed and she slept, nestled trustingly in his arms. Unable to move, he studied her, wondering how he was going to get out of this situation. It would be disastrous if she got the wrong idea.

For a while Dan fought the heavy wave of fatigue that rolled through his exhausted body. But one by one his tense muscles relaxed and he drifted off to sleep.

Sometime in the night, Helen's soft voice roused him.

'Bed,' she murmured.

And too tired to argue, he went, trying not to enjoy the sensation of snuggling up with her and wondering how the hell he was going to tell her that nothing fundamental had changed. He would love the babies. Not her.

'I thought,' she said chattily the next morning, while she was trying to steam the creases from his crumpled suit, 'that under the circumstances it would be wise if we got sorted out early.'

She snatched a quick bite of toast, intending to elaborate, but he forestalled her.

'Sorted…what?'

'Nappies. Clothes. Double buggy. Cots and stuff. What did you think I meant?'

'I don't know. That's why I asked.'

Thrilled with her plans, Helen ploughed on, barely registering the curtness of his tone.

'I'll make a list and start. I'm fit and well now and more able to shop.' She grinned. 'In a few months I won't be able to get behind the steering wheel, let alone squeeze through shop doors. They'll send police outriders ahead of me as a traffic warning.'

He didn't smile. 'Right.'

Helen shot him a quick glance. He looked uptight and had hardly spoken a word, while she'd been yacking on ever since she'd woken up.

'Not worried about the cost of two babies, are you?' she asked anxiously.

'No! Spend what you need.'

He pushed away his virtually uneaten scrambled eggs and stood up. He thought suddenly of Celine and his mind cleared as if by magic. Not the ideal choice to step in his shoes, given her behaviour, but what choice did he have? He needed someone to keep those contracts coming, someone he wouldn't have to train. There simply was no one else.

Yes. He'd lay down conditions. Get their old business relationship back on track. It had been fantastic and could be so again. This, he decided, was no time for personal feelings—he needed a practical solution to the situation, and if he was to stay at Deep Dene then Celine was the obvious candidate for the job. He'd make a point of seeing her today.

'I must go and set some interviews in motion,' he said casually. 'How's the suit doing?'

Taking a moment or two to admire his muscular thighs and long legs, she thought smugly how lovely it was to have Dan there, just in his shirt and tie and underwear and fab legs.

'Not bad. Needs half an hour in the airing cupboard.'

'Thanks,' he said politely. 'And thanks for getting up early to wash my shirt and get it ironed. Appreciated.'

Faintly disconcerted by his manner, she gave a dismissive shrug. 'No problem. Dan—'

'Can't stop. Babies to provide for. Must go and check my e-mails.'

He was out of the kitchen door and halfway to his study before she could close her gaping mouth and say something. Clearing away the dishes, she went over his behaviour with a fine-tooth comb. And decided that he must feel as if he'd collided with a heavy goods vehicle.

She giggled. Her brain was in knots, too! Oh, babies, she thought, you've turned our lives upside down. So much for Dan's sensible plans. She and the babies had shot holes through them.

A short time ago Dan had decided that they'd live separately, and here he was, waking up to the fact that they couldn't stay away from one another. It would take a while for the penny to drop that they were meant to be together, she thought happily. She must give him time to adjust to the new situation.

He rang that evening, to say he'd be late and not to wait up for him. Unexpectedly gnawed by doubts, she finally went to bed around midnight and lay waiting nervously for his return.

A floorboard creaked and she scrambled out of bed, to

find him rummaging in the airing cupboard, a pillow and two blankets on the floor.

'Dan! What are you doing?' she cried in surprise.

He emerged, tousle-haired, a folded sheet in his hand. He looked absolutely exhausted.

'Sorry. Didn't want to wake you,' he muttered. 'Thought I'd make up a bed in the guest room—'

'No,' she said firmly, wrapping her arms around him. Her heart thudded with fear. If he rejected her now, she'd know he'd been with someone else.

The jealousy, the constant uncertainty was terrible. She hated it, but couldn't stop herself from wondering where he'd been—who he'd been with.

His mouth touched her temple but he made no move to hug her in return, his arms dangling by his sides.

'I just need to sleep,' he said wearily. 'I've been interviewing all day—'

'Any luck?' she asked hopefully.

He frowned at his shoes. 'Er…I think so.'

She beamed. 'That's brilliant. You'll be able to ease up—'

'No, Helen. It does mean that I can be here, and you can turn to me whenever you need, but I'll have to work darn hard. Look, let's discuss this in the morning. I'm bushed.'

'Course. But you won't want to be making up a bed.' Bossily she gave him a push towards their bedroom. 'Go on. Get undressed and crawl into ours. Is that your over-night bag?'

'Yup.' He pushed a tired hand over his forehead. 'My suitcase is still in my car.'

'Headache?' she asked sympathetically.

'Mmm.'

'Bed,' she ordered.

And he seemed too shattered to argue. He lay as stiff

as a board, staring up at the ceiling. Helen switched off the lamp and gently stroked his forehead. If he didn't respond, she'd know. He must. Please let him love me, she thought.

'Good?' she enquired softly.

'Mmm.'

Gently her lips touched his temples. She felt him tense up and then in a sudden movement he rolled over and began to kiss her. Delighted, she sank into his arms with relief as he slowly and expertly made love to her.

This was it, she thought, surrendering to the passion that fired every nerve in her body. Dan was on his way back to her.

Sated and utterly content, she lay in his arms dreaming of their future. Gradually she became aware that Dan's muscles were imperceptibly tensing up. Hastily she began to kiss his throat, then his jutting jaw. His teeth were clenched. She tried to soften his mouth with kisses but his lips wouldn't respond.

Slowly her hands wandered up his body in the way he loved.

'Tired,' he said tersely, and rolled away, his tense back preventing any further contact.

Frightened by the rejection, she tried to reason with herself. He *was* tired—beyond exhaustion. Most men wouldn't have been able to make love at all. Only someone as virile as Dan could have found the energy.

So she stroked his hunched shoulder in understanding, biting her lip to stop herself from commenting on the way he flinched from her. He was confused, she reminded herself.

'Sleep,' she said, loving him desperately. And she curled her body against his, wishing that this period of waiting was over and they were normal man and wife again.

When she eventually began to breathe steadily and rhythmically, Dan eased his stiff body from where he'd been perching perilously on the edge of the bed and collected the sheets and blankets he'd abandoned on the landing, throwing them anyhow on the spare bed.

It was inconceivable that he'd broken his promise to himself. Furious with his weakness, he crawled between the crumpled sheets. Helen was very skilled in arousing him. But if he got into the habit of easing his sexual hunger with her, she'd begin to expect more from him than he was prepared to give. So it would have to be the cold shoulder from now on. She'd get the message soon enough.

For a moment he contemplated telling her that he'd taken Celine back as his PA, then decided it would only make Helen hostile. They needed to get on in a civilised, adult way and any mention of Celine would ruin that aim. Even he had mixed feelings about what he'd done.

He set the alarm on his watch. Rose at an ungodly hour, crucified his body with an ice-cold shower in the guest bathroom and pulled on the clothes he'd worn the day before.

He hated not wearing a clean shirt. It reminded him too vividly of being called dirty at school, because his school shirt had had to last a week. And all too clearly he recalled the evening he'd tried to wash it in the bathroom sink. To his horror, he'd discovered it hadn't dried in the morning. The feel of that damp shirt on his skin and the laughter from his class mates would always remain with him.

But painful memories or not, he wasn't going to risk getting a clean shirt from the bedroom and waking Helen.

Taking tea and toast into the study, he switched on his computer and forced himself to redeem his stupidity of the previous night by creating an exemplary database for a national brewery.

Some hours later, the door opened and he heard the pad of Helen's bare feet and the swish of silky material as she crossed the room.

'Gosh!' she cried cheerfully. Too cheerfully for his liking. 'You're up with the lark! Don't know how you have the stamina!'

He didn't turn around. Instead, he continued to stare at his computer screen, though it might as well have been gibberish for all the sense he could make of it.

'It's not a question of stamina. I've got to work.'

'Do you really have to?' she asked gently.

He punched a few keys, frowning at them irritably.

'How the hell else can we survive? Look, is there anything in particular you want? I'm in the middle of something important here.'

The swishing began again, coming nearer. Out of the corner of his eye he could see a long silky skirt in a kind of lemon colour. He could smell her, too. The orange and geranium soap she used. It was interfering with his brain.

'I brought you some tea,' she murmured.

The mug appeared in his line of vision. So did her bare arm, a golden brown from the two weeks of summer weather. He resisted an urge to press his mouth to the soft inside skin and waited while she placed the mug on a clear space above the batch of papers to the left of the keyboard. This action meant she had to stretch forwards and for a brief second or two her body was in close proximity to his. Warm. Softly curved, luring his hands like a Lorelei.

He hardened his resolve and glued his gaze to the monitor.

'Ri-i-ight,' he drawled, as if his mind was elsewhere. And it was.

'I wanted a quick word,' she said breathily.

The back of his neck tingled. He was so very aware of her. The entire length of his body had begun to quiver.

'So long as it *is* quick.'

Busily he tapped in a random figure, knowing he could erase it later.

'I want your undivided attention,' she said with a husky little laugh. 'Shall I pull the plug on you and crash the program, or do I get it?'

Dredging up an irritable grunt, he folded his arms and swivelled his chair around. Somehow he kept his face grim. But inside he was aching to reach out and touch her.

She'd brushed her hair back so that her heart-shaped face could be seen glowing in its full glory, the smoky eyes sultry beneath heavy black lashes, honeyed skin contrasting with pearly teeth as she smiled her irresistible smile.

She wore an eye-bogglingly brief top, rather like the kind Indian women favoured, its scarlet silk just managing to contain some of her magnificent breasts. But not quite. There was enough cleavage and swelling flesh for his hands to twitch rebelliously.

The effort to remain detached made him bark at her.

'Well?'

Her teeth snagged her lip. 'You moved to the spare room,' she said, direct as always.

'I need my sleep.'

He returned to the screen, hoping that would suffice. Her hand pushed back an imaginary strand from his forehead and he felt his body liquidise.

'Didn't you like last night?' she asked provocatively, her hand shaping to the back of his head, travelling to the nape of his neck and stimulating every nerve he possessed.

Dan cursed silently. She wasn't going to take the hint. He'd have to spell it out. Roughly he caught her hand and pushed it away. With difficulty he got up and put several paces between them. And presented her with his back for good measure.

'I'm a man,' he said coldly to the filing cabinet. 'Of course I enjoyed it.'

'Then sleep with me.'

It was all so simple for her. His dark eyes glittered as he turned to glare at her.

'You'd be like a whore to me. Is that what you want?' he asked bluntly.

Her eyes rounded. She took a step back. 'Dan, you know it's not like that—!'

'It is. We agreed what we'd do. We live here separately till the flat—'

'I know, but I thought—'

His irritable stride stopped her in mid-flow. He reached his desk and sat down again. His fingers rested on the keyboard. He pressed the space-bar with an aggressive thumb, the screen-saver disappeared and his client's database filled the screen again.

'I think you've got the wrong idea about us. What happened was a one-off. I needed sex, you were there.'

'Is that all it was?' she asked in indignation.

He ignored the question. 'When the builders have finished the flat, it'll be better for both of us. You can get on with your own life.'

'No, Dan! I want—'

'Helen!' He jerked his head around, fixing her with a hard and direct gaze that held nothing loving in it, nothing affectionate or even lustful. 'I made a mistake last night. This is how I want to live: apart from you. The only way I can live. We must set boundaries and not step over them. We have a past, a sexual past, and it keeps interfering with our new arrangement. But I can't use you like this. I won't sleep with you again. We are not an item any more because you won't trust me and without mutual trust our relationship could never survive. So don't expect anything from me but the courtesy and respect you're due as the mother of my children.'

'That's really how you feel?' she said shakily.

'I can't say it any plainer than that.'

'I see. Thank you. Now I know where I stand.'

He watched the colour drain from her face. And then she walked out; slowly, heavily, as if she carried an unbearable weight. Struggling with a strange, hurting sensation in his chest, he told himself that it was for the best. The last few weeks had been hell. They knew where they stood now and he could devote himself to work and preparing for the babies.

No more sex with Helen. No more temptation. The safety of estrangement beckoned. It was what he wanted. Definitely.

With a sigh he reached for the phone and called Celine.

CHAPTER NINE

IT RAINED for weeks through the late summer and autumn. Helen barely saw Dan, other than when he took her shopping, or on the rare occasions when she asked him to do a job for her.

But every contact was a nightmare: a cocktail of delight and agony, hunger and despair. Between them the atmosphere crackled with static as they fought to remain polite and neutral, while underneath deep and desperate passions flowed.

Dan was presumably anxious that he wouldn't be overcome by any sexual desire, she... She longed to be held by him, to be touched tenderly, to be loved.

Whenever he gazed at her a fraction too long, she held her breath, wondering if he'd break his self-imposed celibacy—or even if he'd give her a friendly hug. None came. He was ruthless with himself and she felt that the chances of their marriage being mended were getting less and less likely.

She tried to goad him. Wore provocative tops, stretched out her long, slender legs, which he'd always worshipped and had loved to kiss from the toes to her thighs in delicious, slow caresses. He merely made his excuses and left.

Tension built up till she could hardly bear to be near him. The urge to reach out and stroke his arm or brush his increasingly dishevelled hair was overwhelming.

Her hands would tremble as they linked together in an effort to stop herself from reaching up to his rigid face and gently stroking away the tautness until it was relaxed and normal again.

But, above all, she missed the feel of him curling around her in bed, missed his sleepy kisses, yearned for his companionship and his physical presence; just being there, silent perhaps, but there. Her husband. The man she loved.

And then they were all alone. The builders finished the flat and said their farewells, presenting them both with flowers and wine, kisses and handshakes. That made them smile for a short time afterwards, but soon their faces returned to their habitual frozen politeness.

The house looked fabulous, as Dan had predicted, the stunning reception rooms beautifully furnished and decorated, the light pouring in from carefully restored windows onto the polished oak floors with their thick Persian rugs and gleaming antique furniture, silverware and expensive oil paintings.

And for what? So they had a perfect home, the house of their dreams, a garden to die for. But its sheer perfection emphasised the emptiness of her personal life.

What fun would it be, to swim in the pool alone, never to splash Dan and squeal when he tried to duck her? Who would join her in the vicious, hilarious games of croquet they'd originally planned on the vast lawn, or, as Dan had threatened, thrash her at tennis on the purpose-built court?

People must envy her. If they only knew!

In the middle of an ante-natal class in the nearby town of Lewes, Helen stared moodily at her huge twenty-six-week bump—which other people kept telling her was hardly worthy of the name 'bump' at all—and finally acknowledged the fact that Dan wasn't likely even to fancy her any more. Despite what everyone thought about her figure, her Mata Hari days were over and in her eyes she had taken on the appearance of a barrage balloon.

He'd made it clear that he didn't love her. And now he'd have lost any interest in her physically. *If* he ever stayed around, it would be for the sake of the babies. And she wasn't sure that was a good enough reason.

On the mat beside her, the red-haired Kirsty was practising her breathing, assisted by her milkman husband Tom. They giggled a lot and touched a lot and looked at one another all the time as if the world were contained solely in the space around them.

That was how it should be for her, Helen thought sadly.

'When's your old man coming here, then?' whispered Kirsty between panting breaths. 'I'm dying to get up close and personal with him. He's a hunk. I saw him drop you this evening and begged the Fates to make him stop but they must have been engaged on another line.'

Helen found a weak smile in response. She liked Kirsty very much and only Tom's constant attention had made her hesitate to intrude and ask Kirsty if they could meet up for lunch one day.

'Dan's self-employed. He's got into the habit of working twenty-four hours a day and doesn't know how to stop,' she explained, evading the issue.

When the class had been wound up and Tom went to get their raincoats, Kirsty hesitantly touched Helen's arm.

'Don't think I'm interfering, but...do get your Dan to come. You need a husband's support more than any of us,' she urged. 'Tell him money isn't as important as personal support. Tom offered to take on another job to help make ends meet, but I said we'd manage. I'd rather he did his milk round and came home early as he does, giving me cuddles and cups of tea!'

Helen smiled again, this time rather wistfully. 'I'll mention it when he collects me. Look...I'd like us to meet up somewhere. Can we have lunch some time?'

'Great!' Kirsty enthused. 'It's getting boring being at home so much because of all this rain. I've forgotten what summer was like, it was so brief. Thank heavens we live on a hill, or we'd be flooded. What about you, any trouble with the floods?'

'Fortunately we're on a rise, too,' Helen replied. 'The village has been cut off twice because the river burst its banks and our lane was impassable for a while. If Dan hadn't bought a four-wheel drive we'd be in serious trouble, stuck out miles from anywhere.'

'Tell you what,' Kirsty said, 'it's Bonfire Night in two weeks' time. Our flat overlooks the High Street in Lewes and it gets a brilliant view of the procession. Have you ever been to the celebrations?'

Helen had certainly heard of the famous Bonfire Night there. Thousands flocked to the small market town to mark the fifth of November when Guy Fawkes had tried to blow up the Houses of Parliament and the King of England, some four hundred years earlier. And by all accounts, the event was spectacular.

'No— Dan's always longed to, but we've never found the time—'

'Then find it,' Kirsty said firmly. 'With twins in the offing, it'll be the last chance you have of behaving like normal adults on Bonfire Night for years and years! Come to us, both of you. Bring a bottle and a packet of crisps or something. It's a fantastic sight. Tom's a Bonfire Boy—'

'A what?' Helen giggled.

Conscious that the caretaker was hovering and hoping to lock up, they moved outside and stood in the porch.

'There are loads of local bonfire societies,' Tom explained enthusiastically. 'You join up and pay a subscription and hold money-making events, then your society has its own bonfire with elaborate displays. You make collections on the night and all the money goes to charity—'

'And you get to wear a costume,' Kirsty said, her eyes twinkling. 'Tom's a pirate. Junior will be enrolled from

birth if they can find an eye patch small enough. Honestly,
you must come. It's an amazing sight. You should see the
Zulu warriors! You'll never forget it. The whole street is
filled with burning torches for as far as you can see and
they roll blazing tar barrels down the road and there are
fabulous bands—'

'What about the rain?' Helen asked doubtfully.

'They march whatever. Maybe it'll ease up by then.
We've got two weeks, after all,' Kirsty said. 'Please
come!'

'I'd love to,' Helen said on impulse. It would do her
good. Get her out of herself. Though Dan would never
come. 'I'm not sure how Dan's fixed, but maybe he'd take
time off and come, too.'

'Right. Be in Lewes before six p.m. because they close
the town. Park off the street for safety. There'll be
thousands and thousands of people milling around. We can
watch in comfort from our window. Here's our address.'
She scribbled on a piece of paper and handed it over.
'Must dash. See you!'

Helen waved goodbye, quite excited by the event. Soon
after they'd arrived, the workmen had told her about the
extraordinary celebrations, the huge bonfires, fantastic fire-
work displays and set pieces—usually depicting somebody
who'd been slated or exposed in some way by the news-
papers. The builders' enthusiasm had spilled over to her
and she and Dan had been very keen to go one day.

When the car drew up, she could hardly wait to tell him
that she was going.

'All right?' he asked with his usual cool detachment.

'I am. Feeling great, actually.'

He flicked a glance at her face and she realised from
his surprised expression that she hadn't been this animated
for ages.

'The class was that good?'

She gave a small chuckle. 'Oh, not the panting and stuff. No, I've made friends with one of the mums. Kirsty. She and her husband Tom have asked if I'd like to watch the Bonfire Parade from their window in Lewes High Street on the fifth. They have a fabulous view. It's an unmissable opportunity.'

'You're going alone?'

'Definitely. It'll be the last chance I have till the babies are nine or ten years old.'

He frowned. 'You're planning on driving there on your own, and coming back late at night?'

'That's the idea.'

'I don't think that's wise.'

'I'm going, Dan,' she said calmly. 'Are you going to chain me to the stove?'

His brows got closer and closer together. 'I'd better give you a lift and return later to collect you.'

'No, they close the town. If you're worried about me being out late at night, then you'll have to come with me. Kirsty won't mind, she's been dying to meet you,' she said. 'Don't worry, you won't have to sit around with us. Once you've done the polite chat for a short time, you can disappear for a few hours. Tom's in the parade, so he won't be there, either. We two women can have a good natter. Do what you like, Dan. I'm going and that's that.'

He grunted and seemed to be struggling with his interest in the procession and the ghastly thought of having to spend time with her.

'All right,' he muttered. 'You've given me no choice.'

Helen felt nervous about having Dan around her, even for a short time during the evening. All sexual tension had now vanished. They'd been so cold towards one another lately that she wasn't sure she could stand his glacial comments. The last time they'd been shopping, she reckoned she could have cut the atmosphere with a cushion.

In silence they drove through the rain, the headlights illuminating flooded fields everywhere. Dan seemed tense and annoyed, as if he resented her for forcing him to go with her on Bonfire Night.

He opened the front door of Deep Dene and, as usual, paused to politely enquire, 'Anything you need?'

'No, thanks. I'm whacked. All that panting and huffing. I'm going to bed,' she replied, rubbing her spine.

'Problem with your back?' he asked.

'A bit.' She gave a rueful sigh. 'Not surprising, when you think of what it's having to support. If I didn't know different, I'd say there was a cartload of monkeys in my tummy.'

Frozen-faced, Dan turned away. 'See you tomorrow. Sleep well.'

'Goodnight,' she said in a forlorn little voice.

He hesitated, then, screwed up with tension, he strode quickly to his flat and went straight to his computer. As it whirred into action he wished he could have placed his hand on her abdomen and felt the babies moving. He was desperate to feel close to them. But he dared not touch her.

The last few weeks had been a trial of strength that he'd almost lost on several occasions. He was now so wound up with desire that he'd kept all contact to the bare minimum, punishing himself with cold showers, press-ups, fierce dedication to work and near rudeness to Helen.

None of that helped much. He still felt a knee-jerk response whenever he clapped eyes on her. Still wanted to tuck her into his shoulder and stroke her slender back, murmur wicked things in her ear and hear her giggle saucily as she did unspeakably erotic things to him. Sex was the very devil to control once it had been enjoyed.

There was something wonderfully sensual about Helen at the moment. The Empire line red wool dress flattered and concealed, and, despite proclaiming that she waddled like a duck with chronic corns, she moved gracefully, carrying her pregnancy with pride.

Everything about her was soft and tempting. And he'd just elected to spend a good chunk of an evening with her in a couple of weeks! He groaned and decided to get out on the streets to watch the parade as soon as he decently could.

In the bedroom above he could hear her moving about. He sat staring at the monitor, aching for her. He couldn't hack it. Even this limited 'togetherness' was destroying him inch by inch. If it weren't for the babies, he'd have been off and halfway around the world.

And then came a crash and a simultaneous scream.

He was out of his flat and bounding up the stairs three at a time before he even drew breath.

'Helen! I'm coming!' he yelled.

Expecting the worst, nevertheless he felt a lurch in his chest when he saw her lying flat on the floor, a small occasional table overturned by her feet, ornaments and photographs scattered on the carpet.

'Don't move!' he said urgently. 'I'll get an ambulance—'

'No, for heaven's sake, don't!' she cried, sitting up abruptly, her hair flying about her embarrassed face. Heartbreakingly beautiful. 'I didn't fall, Dan. I was lying down *already*. I'm OK, honest. Please go. Let me roll myself up in my own good time. I hate you seeing me so clumsy.'

She was virtually naked, he realised, just a gaping satin wrap slithering erotically around her body. He gulped, overcome, his limbs suddenly heavy, brain slowing, breathing rapid, mouth dry...the usual signs. Damn.

'Why were you lying down?' he groused.

She looked at him in wry amusement, her eyes bright, her mouth apologetic.

'I was doing leg circles,' she explained. 'And I circled a bit too vigorously and knocked over the table. I'm terribly sorry to drag you up here for no reason at all. I'm so clumsy—'

'No. Not clumsy.' He was having difficulty getting the words out. They sounded stilted and unsympathetic. He tried harder. 'Are you sure you're not hurt?'

'No!' She gave a rueful laugh. 'Only my pride. I screamed because the crash sounded so loud. It gave me a shock. I'm unhurt, honestly—'

'Will you...will you be all right? The babies, I mean?' he muttered.

Her hand went to her abdomen. Laughing grey eyes met his and he was drawn into their smoky depths.

'They're doing leg circles, too,' she said softly. 'Feel.'

'I...don't think...'

'Stop thinking, Dan, and do what you want to,' she coaxed. 'These are your babies. Say hello.'

If she did but know it, he said 'hello' to them every time he saw Helen. But...he did want to feel them move. Desperately.

Fiercely controlling his delight, he put on the kind of concerned attitude a doctor might adopt and tentatively let his palm come to rest where she'd indicated.

Something—a hand, a foot—jabbed angrily at his hand and he jerked it away in alarm before replacing it.

Small bumps appeared at random, disturbing the smooth and gentle swell of Helen's abdomen. His heart melted with love. Gently he stroked the silky skin and, lost in wonder, bent to kiss it.

Hello, babies, he said silently. Your father here. Hello, little ones. Hello, my loves. I'll be a good father. Promise. Will love you with all my heart.

His mouth nuzzled softly, the warm sweetness of her infusing his lips with tantalising tastes. He put his cheek against her abdomen and stroked her lovingly while she coiled his hair in her fingers.

The amazing fact that he and Helen had been part of the creation of these tiny lives made his heart lurch. Awed, he slowly kissed every inch of her belly, silently repeating his promise to his babies that he would love and care for them all his life.

My darling, precious babies.

He was overcome with emotion. It flowed through him like a river, melting bone and sinew, and resolution alike. And somehow her arms had wound around him and she was sighing and he was exploring further, gently caressing her breasts, touching them with a lightly questing finger, his dark, glowing eyes mesmerised by the dark-centred nipples.

She shrugged off the wrap. Her mouth was on his and they kissed with a long, lazy thoroughness that tantalised more than any fast and fevered passion. This was adoration. This was worship.

With great care he let his lips brush her blissfully closed lids, his hands cradling her upturned face in awe.

Mother of his children, he thought hazily. And he had felt them move as if welcoming him—though they were quiescent now, perhaps sleeping. He shook with the wonder of it, needed to keep on kissing her to ease the huge lump of emotion that was stuck in his gullet.

It would be a complete tour of her body. His mouth would know every inch. His hands would follow. He needed to remember Helen in exquisite detail when he was alone.

Unexpectedly, she began to remove his clothes. Gradually he felt himself being swallowed by something dark and wonderful, drowning in a whirlpool of sensuality, her skin hot now, her body trembling, groans of need whispering from her lips.

'Make love to me,' she breathed into his ear.

He raised drugged and harrowed eyes. 'No, Helen! No! I...hadn't meant...'

'Too late,' she murmured.

'I was only...'

It seemed impossible for him to say more than a few words before his throat closed up.

'I know. But these things happen,' she whispered into his mouth.

Wanting their union, he groaned and did his best to resist.

'It—it was the emotion of the moment. Feeling the babies move beneath my fingers. It was...amazing.'

'And we've been wanting to touch one another for weeks,' she said candidly.

Perceptive woman. Had it been that obvious? Had she seen the wealth of longing in his eyes, the desperate efforts he was making to stop himself from touching her?

'It's...not a good idea—'

'To hell with good ideas,' she husked.

He groaned. 'I...can't.'

'I think you can,' she said, placing her hand on his groin, and he felt himself leap to her touch, hard and throbbing. 'Proof positive. I want you, too, Dan.'

He could have drawn back then. Just. But she kissed him artfully, curling her tongue around his, moving her breasts against his chest so seductively that his iron will was broken.

His mouth tasted her sweetness. His body became master of his head. 'Is it still safe for you?' he asked hoarsely.

'Be gentle. Please. Probably our last time.'

He disguised his choking cry by kissing her hard. Then with infinite care he drew her onto his lap. His pregnant wife. The woman he'd once surrendered to, had viewed as the one person who could save him from a life of in-hibition and a lack of love—and who had failed him.

Though he still wanted her.

Last time, he told himself. And let his tongue coil around hers, invading her mouth, her eager response sending him over the edge and into the world of pure sensation he'd never thought he'd know again.

An extraordinary thrill claimed his entire nervous system, charging it with electric tremors that rippled through him over and over again. The silk of her skin, her frantic little moans, all conspired to intensify his pleasure as he devoted himself to arousing her in a languorous and complete dedication to the woman who carried his children.

Goodbye, Helen, he thought with a lump in his throat as she shuddered and swayed against him. And then he lost himself in the slow, powerful build-up to his climax, abandoning for a while the certain knowledge that this was the end of it all and from now on they would become as strangers to one another.

He wanted this to last for ever. Did everything he could to ensure it did, postponing the moment when cold reality would hit him and he would be her estranged husband once more.

But her movements foiled his plan and he felt himself spiral up to another plane, hover in a prolonged, sweetly pained ecstasy, and then float back down again. Helen slumped against him, spent, as replete as he. And suddenly hurting somewhere in his chest, he withdrew from her arms, looking into her drowsy, slaty eyes.

'Rub my back,' she mumbled sleepily.

Breathing hard, he turned her around and pulled her buttocks against his pelvis, his fingers working the muscles of her back with a rhythm that was highly arousing for him. So he moved away.

'What is it?' she asked softly.

He couldn't bear it any longer. This way of living was destroying him inch by inch. There was only one solution. He felt the hot pricking of tears and willed them to retreat.

'Dan! You're frightening me! Don't look like that,' Helen pleaded, kissing his mouth. He jerked away. 'We've not done anything wrong. We're married—'

'That's just it, Helen,' he said harshly. 'We're living a farce and I can't stand it any longer. We can't stay married. We must make a clean break. It's not right that we keep easing our sexual needs with one another.'

'But—!'

'I don't want to listen to anything you have to say!' he lashed, his eyes blazing with anger. 'All the time we're hitched up like this, we might as well be shackled. I want out. As soon as possible.' He mustn't weaken. Mustn't let her dismayed face sway him. 'Then maybe we'll treat one another like acquaintances, instead of potential sex objects.'

She swallowed, the pain all too visible in her limpid grey eyes. 'Sex,' she said bitterly, 'has a hell of a lot to answer for.'

'So we take it out of the equation. I will be a lodger and the father of your children.' He clenched his teeth together hard and came out with something to clinch his argument, something that would drive home to her what he intended. 'If I need sex, then I will go elsewhere.'

'I thought you had,' she flung, clearly hurt.

He gave a noncommittal shrug. What did it matter what she thought?

'I'll see a solicitor in the morning.'

With a hastily stifled gasp, she dragged on her robe, her huge grey eyes fixed on his granite face.

'Take me along, too. I will need a—a s-solicitor,' she stumbled. 'I'll cite your adultery with Celine, of course.'

He tensed and then realised the futility of any explanation. Better this way. Better for his sanity. With a curt nod, he turned away, picking up his clothes.

'I won't contest it,' he croaked. And walked out. Unsteadily, but he managed it.

So he'd admitted it at last, she thought miserably. After all his protestations of innocence, his expressions of injured pride, he'd finally realised that he couldn't deny his infidelity any longer.

Her heart felt as if it had been emptied of all emotion. Dan had lied and lied to her—perhaps he'd done so for a long time.

Had Dan latched on to her all those years ago purely for security? She knew how awful his upbringing had been. Perhaps he'd needed a comfort blanket. And also was physically in need of someone he could eventually possess as his convenient bed-partner. It had been sheer sexual need all the time. That and the safety of someone he knew.

All this time she'd imagined that he loved her deep down, and that he'd come back to her because they were meant for one another. It had all been in her head. She'd been the one in love, not Dan. She'd adored the ground he walked on, but he…he'd used her to fill a more basic need.

Someone he could trust. Someone he could have sex with.

Dan hadn't ever wanted her as his wife and partner, someone to love. But he *had* needed to satisfy his lust. And he had needed a haven for his wounded soul.

She…she'd been someone safe and unthreatening. Good old Helen, fine for a roll in the hay but not good enough to love!

Well, *rot* him! She'd live very well without him! He wasn't worth worrying about! He'd soon see that she didn't need him, that she could function perfectly well on her own, with the twins.

They'd see him, but on her terms. Not with Celine, for instance. At the solicitors in the morning, she'd make darn sure of that.

Crawling out of bed late, she discovered that he'd left a note saying he'd be out till four p.m. and that she was to ring him if necessary. The note wasn't even signed and the pencil strokes were hard and fierce, the writing erratic as if anger and hatred had driven every word.

She snorted. She'd only ring if the house was burning down around her and a horde of escaped murderers brandishing cutlasses were banging on the door.

And from then on, she made a point of keeping out of his way—while he seemed to be doing exactly the same thing. They were completely estranged, communicating only by phone or by note.

She felt bitter and badly used. And very unhappy that there was nothing that would bring back the man she'd thought she'd married.

CHAPTER TEN

ON THE morning of November the fifth, the rain eased at last. Helen went for a walk, though she felt a little woozy and soon made her way back, deciding to save her energy for the fun of the evening. Dan surprised her by calling in on his return, to say that he'd have the car outside at five-fifteen—apparently he was still intending to go to the Bonfire Night Parade. Amazing.

Conversation during the drive to Lewes was desultory. Neither of them referred to what had happened when they'd last been together and had made love. Helen could hardly believe it herself.

She heaved in a shuddering breath, remembering. He had spent hours just kissing and touching her. She'd never known that there was such an intensity of latent pleasure in her body. There had been something sweetly and painfully poignant about the way they'd explored one another...as if they'd never really known what their bodies were like.

And now every pore of him was emblazoned in her mind. The difference in muscle tones, the thinness of skin over bone, the tension that ripped through him when her teeth grazed gently at his flesh.

It would have been wonderful if only he had loved her, too, instead of seeing her as a convenience. What an idiot she'd been. Dan would never have stayed with her if he hadn't been so wary of rejection from other women.

He'd kept up the relationship merely because the alternative was too unnerving for him. He got good sex—or he had done, until they'd both started working so hard—

and he was relieved that he had a wife he felt comfortable with.

Huh. Helen glared. It wasn't the basis for a good marriage. No wonder he'd strayed when Celine had joggled her bosom at him.

'Here we are. You jump out, I'll watch you in then go and park the car.'

'Right,' she said crossly, annoyed by his curtness.

This temporary 'togetherness' was a sham. She hated it. But they had to go through with it this evening. Already the divorce was under way. She winced.

'Hurry up,' he said irritably. 'I'm holding up the traffic.'

'I'm hugely pregnant, they'll have to wait!' She paused. 'Dan…you'll be nice for Kirsty and Tom, won't you?' she asked warily.

His profile hardened. 'I won't let you down.'

Relieved, she hurried to the flat door and rang the bell. Tom answered, apologised for the stairs she'd have to climb and guided her up to the first floor where she was hugged by Kirsty.

The living room was tiny but decorated with flair and imagination. There were photos of Kirsty and her husband Tom everywhere, and of her parents, brothers, sisters, his brothers and sisters and parents…not a surface seemed to be without a collection of lovingly arranged frames and smiling faces. Kirsty showed Helen around with pride and they chatted for a while before the doorbell rang and Dan was let in.

'It's very homely,' he said quietly, after Kirsty had invited him to sit in one of the threadbare armchairs.

Kirsty made a face. 'You mean it's tatty,' she teased.

'No. I mean homely. Somewhere you'd want to come back to.'

'Flatterer,' said Kirsty, but she beamed with pleasure. 'All done on a shoestring, I can assure you.'

Dan's eyes were thoughtful. 'What does Tom do?'

'He's a milkman.' Kirsty's face was soft and loving as she fondled a photo of Tom. 'It's lovely. He gets up when I'm fast asleep, works a full day and yet still comes home mid-afternoon.'

Helen gulped. She wanted that kind of affection very badly. For some reason, being here only made her situation harder to bear.

'We've brought you a present. For the baby.' Gruff and diffident, Dan pulled a small and beautifully wrapped packet from his pocket. Helen's eyes widened. She didn't know anything about this. How thoughtful. She met Dan's eyes and her face softened in gratitude. 'Just a token to say thanks for giving us a grandstand seat,' he said.

'Thank you! I wasn't expecting…' Kirsty's voice trailed away as the wrapping paper fell away to reveal a cute white and navy spotted outfit. 'It's gorgeous!' she cried, bending to kiss Helen and then Dan. 'From Tot's!' she gasped, reading the label.

'I hope you haven't got one like it already,' ventured Dan, warily.

'Are you joking? Me, buy stuff from Tot's? Junior will be in hand-me-downs or second-hand stuff. He won't know what he's wearing, after all. He's sleeping in a drawer till he's big enough for my sister's cot. And she's handing over her buggy any day now. We decided to co-ordinate our kids and take turns with equipment, you see!'

Dan chuckled, warmth suddenly relaxing his tense face.

'Your baby is very lucky to have you and Tom as its parents,' he said easily.

Kirsty batted her eyelashes at him. 'A charmer as well as a hunk!' she declared and whispered loudly, pseudo *sotto voce*, 'I will seriously have to consider you for the father of my next child!'

They all laughed, the ice broken, though Helen's laugh was hollow and forced. It pained her to think of the children he would father by another woman one day. Because whether he was wary of being hurt or not, he'd be snapped up pretty darn quick.

Upset, she fell silent, explaining away her reticence by saying she was feeling tired—which was true.

To be polite, Dan asked about Kirsty's extended family and she happily explained the huge ramifications of her family tree while they munched on sandwiches and watched the crowds building up outside in the High Street.

Despite her preoccupation with her loverless future, Helen found herself enthralled when the procession started. Kirsty tried to point out Tom but the blazing torches were so bright that it was hard to identify him. Dan was nowhere to be seen. He'd stayed around for a while, behaving like an attentive husband should, and had then gone walkabout in the crowd.

She shifted uncomfortably in her seat. Her back was aching a lot now. And the pain had moved around to the front. She began to feel worried. By ten o'clock the ache was stronger, and hitting her in more and more frequent waves. She was relieved when Dan returned and they could say their goodbyes.

'Hold my arm,' she said, a catch in her breath as they walked to where he'd parked the car.

'You look very pale. Rather drawn. Something's wrong, isn't it?' he asked, his eyes narrowed.

'Yes. It is. I have a pain,' she answered as calmly as she could.

He frowned warily, his gaze now piercing. 'What sort of a pain?' he demanded.

'I think,' she said, suddenly frightened, 'that it's the kind of pain that ought to be investigated.'

Dan swore under his breath, hooked an arm around her and guided her to the car.

'It'll be quicker if I drive to the hospital, rather than call an ambulance,' he said tersely, feeding her into the passenger seat with great care. He raced around to the driver's side and flung the car into gear. His hand briefly enclosed hers, big, warm and security itself. 'Don't be afraid. I'll look after you. Now you ring the hospital and get them on stand-by. I've already programmed the number in, in case of any problem. It's on the menu. Can you manage that?'

'Yes.'

Surprised and oddly comforted that he'd thought so far ahead, she found the number and dialled. He was already forging a way around the back streets and heading out of the town for Brighton.

'Well done,' he said abruptly, when she'd made the call. 'Tell me what the pain is like. And how you feel. No being brave, now. The truth.'

'I thought it was just a backache. A kind of dull ache. It wasn't painful but just sort of there, all the time. And then it started to come and go and it got worse this evening and now it's here,' she said, holding her tummy. 'And it comes more strongly than before, then goes again. I'm frightened, Dan. I don't want to lose the babies!'

His big hand grasped hers tightly and then let go. 'You won't. We'll get you seen to. It'll be a false alarm.' He threw her a shaky grin, which she knew was false because it wavered. 'Indigestion. Kirsty's tuna sandwiches, perhaps.'

'Yes. Course,' she agreed.

But she knew it was more serious. And she felt more scared than she'd ever been in her whole life.

'If it's a urinary infection as they say,' argued Dan more than an hour later, 'they'll get it under control easily. You know the babies are OK, we saw that on the ultrasound—'

'But they said the infection could start off labour!'

Alone now with Dan in the dimly lit room, Helen felt cold and utterly terrified. She could see that Dan's face was pale and he looked as harrowed as she felt. He was doing his best to cheer her up but she knew how strong the contractions were and the painkillers and antibiotics weren't helping.

'If that happens, then you're in the best place,' he reasoned.

She wanted a cuddle, not wisdom. But he sat rigidly a few feet away as if they were commuters on the train to London.

'I'm twenty-eight weeks, Dan!' she moaned. 'I'm supposed to go to forty! And now they've pumped steroids into me to help if the babies come prematurely and I'm full of horrible drugs which I never, ever wanted, and I feel *sick*.'

'What can I do to help? Tell me. Anything.'

'Get the babies on your mobile. Say I'm not ready,' she muttered, bringing a faint smile to his anxious face. 'I'm sorry to whine, Dan. It's just that this isn't how I imagined it.'

'Life never is,' he said quietly, his eyes remote.

No. She'd learnt that in the past few months. 'Help me off this wretched bed, will you, please? I need the loo.'

Dan left her to the ministrations of the midwife. It gave him a moment to gather himself together. He was confused by his feelings—unsure whether he was afraid for Helen's sake, or for the safety of his children. His mind seemed to be having difficulty touching base. Terror had taken over. This wasn't a time for deep thinking.

He looked up as Helen and the midwife returned a

lot faster than they'd left, Helen's expression one of sheer panic.

'Oh, Dan! The babies might be coming!' she cried shakily.

And he took her awkwardly in his arms. 'If they do, they'll be fine. Tough stock. Great parents,' he murmured in her ear. And all the time his heart was screaming in despair. It was too early. How could they survive? And Helen... 'Don't worry,' he forced out somehow, in a reasonably calm voice. 'They've got everything in hand.'

People arrived from everywhere. Helen was examined, phone calls were made. Dan watched the activity with growing alarm.

'What's the matter?' he demanded. 'Why aren't you moving her to the labour ward *now*?'

'We can't. We need two incubators in case, *in case*, I emphasise, the babies are born,' the midwife said, her measured tones belying her harassed expression. 'We're just organising them.'

'Upstairs?' Dan said, suddenly reading more into the midwife's words than he liked.

'No. We don't have any spare,' she admitted.

Helen gasped. 'My babies!' she whimpered, holding her abdomen defensively.

'It's all right,' the midwife said calmly. 'We're phoning round.'

'Who? Where?' Dan shot, ready to knock heads together if necessary.

'The registrar's sorting it now. There's a national computer that shows available beds and incubators and we'll know in two ticks. Now.' The midwife turned to the terrified Helen. 'Let's put you on a drip and we'll be all ready.'

'For where?' growled Dan, eyebrows glowering.

The midwife didn't seem phased. Presumably this was

a common occurrence. 'Could be Scotland, Birmingham, or possibly Plymouth or the Isle of Wight.'

Helen's mouth fell open. *'What?!'* she shrieked.

'No panic, I assure you. There'll be plenty of time for you to get to your designated hospital,' the midwife soothed.

'But...all those places are *miles* away! We'd have to stay overnight!' she cried, aghast. 'Dan! You don't even have a change of shirt—'

'It doesn't matter,' he said gently, amused by her concern for him at a time like this. 'It's not important.'

And Helen stared at him in amazement. 'Not...important?'

'No. I know what *is* important now. And it's certainly not a clean shirt.'

He smiled at her, his fingers briefly caressing her upturned face, and she persuaded her lips to wiggle a little in a pathetic attempt to smile back.

The midwife sat next to her and took her hand. Dan saw that it trembled and his heart went out to her.

'Helen, if the babies are born prematurely, then they'll be in hospital for quite a while. You and your husband will be able to stay—there are bedrooms put aside for such eventualities. Not Ritz standards, but adequate. Or does your husband have work commitments he can't get out of—?'

'No, I don't,' Dan said quickly, stroking Helen's hair. She leaned into him and he felt her relax a little against his thumping heart. He'd stay a year if necessary. 'I can put my work on hold for as long as it takes, wherever you send us.'

He didn't care. His precious business could go hang if it meant that Helen and his babies were all right.

'Good.' The midwife smiled. 'You'll be a great comfort to your wife. Now, the babies might not be born now at all, of course, but if they are, then they'll remain in the hospital till they're fit enough to be transferred to a hospital nearer to you. OK?'

'How long might it be before they come back to Sussex?' Helen asked tremulously.

'I can't say. It depends on their birth weight and how they progress. But it could be three months before they're home with you.'

'Three *months*!' she gasped in horror.

Dan felt his stomach flip over. This was a nightmare.

'Now,' the midwife said breezily, 'remember this is only *if* they are born. You might be sent home intact after a little while, with instructions to take it easy and come back in January.'

Dan choked back a groan and began to pace up and down, trying furiously to hide his fears. With every fibre of his being he hoped this was a false alarm. It was unbelievable that Helen could give birth safely, so early. The twins would have been small under normal circumstances, but now...

He felt tears filling his eyes and brutally held them back. Helen needed him. She must be going through all kinds of hell.

Appalled at the situation, he took her hand and managed to smile at her petrified face.

'One thing I insist on,' he said solemnly, somehow summoning up a twinkle in his eye. 'On no account is any child of mine to be called Guy just because it's Bonfire Night. Or Catherine Wheel. OK?'

'OK.' She produced a weak smile and squeezed his hand so hard that it hurt. 'Scotland would be a nice place to be born,' she said shakily. 'Lovely scenery.'

'Yes,' he agreed, going along with her attempt at levity. 'Personally, I'm torn. The idea of the Isle of Wight appeals—though Birmingham's good for shopping—'

Her mouth wobbled and he saw with dismay that she was close to tears. 'Oh, Dan! Why can't we stay here? Scotland's so f-far away—'

'Portsmouth!' announced the registrar, poking her head around the door. *'Now.'*

A trolley. Being wheeled through Accident and Emergency at a smart lick to a waiting ambulance. A gale whipping Dan's hair everywhere, blowing so hard that it seemed to be trying to stop him from climbing in after the trolley-stretcher. Torrential rain, making driving conditions treacherous.

The paramedics were worrying quietly about the floods, taking two diversions on the way. The blue light flashed as they screamed along the road, devouring miles in a third of the time it normally took to get to Portsmouth. The doctor monitored her, worryingly accompanying them in the ambulance, in case Helen gave birth before they reached the hospital.

They kept the banter going, telling jokes to relax them both, to stop their jittering teeth and trembling hands and to briefly change the looks of stunned horror on their faces.

'Lunch and duty frees will be served by cabin staff,' announced the paramedic with a grin. And later... 'This is your Captain speaking. We're flying at five feet, at a speed of—ah. Er, yes. Better keep quiet about that or we'll be nabbed by the cops. Now, if you look to your right, you'll see Paris, and on your left is Timbuktu. Estimated time of arrival...'

They both managed weak smiles. Anything rather than what they really felt like doing: yelling in despair, crying...

A chirpy midwife came to meet them at the hospital and she was calm and casual as if this was an everyday occurrence. It was a quiet, private room. They administered yet more drugs for Helen to stop the contractions. Mercifully she slept.

Dan couldn't. Restless and agitated, he rang her parents and made light of it all, adopting the same merry tone as the midwife. Two a.m. He paced the floor relentlessly, blessing the vending machine that kept him topped up with caffeine.

Later that morning there were more steroid injections for Helen and an internal examination. What could he do? If only he could have had a medical career he would have taken charge then and there.

As it was, he felt helpless. As useless as a rice pudding. His only role was to pat Helen's hand and tell her that she'd be all right. As if the hell he knew. Neither of them believed it, anyway.

'Well,' said the doctor an hour later, 'your children are refusing to do what they're told. They're determined to be born before Christmas and see the New Year in. They're on their way, Helen, and they'll be born by tonight.'

'Tonight!' they both gasped in dismay.

His arm came protectively around Helen. She buried her face in him, her body trembling pathetically. The dangers united them, he thought in misery. He held her close, afraid to let her go, clinging onto their moments together.

'Definite. We'll wait till the contractions are stronger and then we'll whip you in for a Caesarean. A nice little bikini cut for a nice little bikini.'

Helen scowled. 'Huh! Some hopes! I'll never wear one again!'

'Oh, you will. And I bet she looks fantastic in one, doesn't she, Dan?'

'Mega,' he croaked, fear clutching at his loins.

'There!' said the doctor with satisfaction. 'I knew it. Don't worry about a thing. Piece of cake, Helen. You'll wake up and it'll all be over.'

Dan felt his hand being crushed. 'Piece of cake?' she complained crossly. 'You have the babies, then!'

The doctor looked abashed. 'You'll be OK,' he said gently. 'Honest.'

'And how dangerous will it be for the twins?' Helen asked in a small, scared little voice.

'They'll be tiny and will need a lot of care, but we've done this umpteen times before. Don't worry. Relax. Rest as much as you can. Dan, Nurse will take you to the prem unit.'

'No,' he said shortly, glaring at the doctor who seemed determined to part them. 'I don't want to leave my wife—'

'But she needs to sleep. She's fighting it and she needs all the rest she can get. Nothing's going to happen for a while.'

'Helen?' he asked.

'I am tired,' she admitted. 'Sleep would be lovely.'

'You won't take her away?' he said to the doctor suspiciously.

'No. Ages to go yet. Let your wife sleep.'

Too numb to argue but reluctant to leave Helen, he saw the sense in leaving her alone. He knew his agitation would only communicate itself to her and she'd be unable to give in to her need for sleep.

Letting go of her hand was tough. At the door he turned to look at Helen but her eyes were already closed. Suddenly he felt alone. Shut out. She and the babies had each other, linked physically by a tie far greater than any contribution he'd made.

And she and the babies would go through this together while he sat on the sidelines, waiting, worrying, totally cut off from them.

The nurse coughed discreetly and he followed her, walking on legs of jelly to the intensive care baby unit. It was like getting into Fort Knox. Eventually they were allowed in and he was 'gowned up'.

There were two empty incubators in the unit. Looking at them, imagining his babies in there, Dan felt emotion shake his self-control, the reality of it all coming home to him.

Somewhere in the background, the nurse was trying to reassure him with her cheery voice and air of efficiency. It was all very well for her. These weren't her babies. It wasn't her partner who was going through an emergency operation. Her children weren't going to be so undeveloped that they'd be linked up to wires and machines the moment they were born.

He flinched. They'd be so small. So helpless. And those machines seemed brutal.

Shaking, sweltering in the heat, he wrinkled his nose at the clinical smell. Everywhere he looked in the barely lit room there were incubators, and batteries of alarming machines. *Star Trek* stuff.

'There's one nurse per incubator and several doctors on the ward. After the ICU—Intensive Care Unit—they're moved to the high dependency unit, still on monitors. We'll show your wife a video of all this so she has an idea—'

'Good grief!' he breathed in astonishment, glimpsing at a red, hairy and pathetically scrawny little baby in a nearby incubator. His heart contracted with compassion. If this were his child he'd be going crazy with worry. He felt suddenly sick. 'How…how old is that kiddie?'

'A day,' the nurse said gently. 'She's only one pound in weight, though she's doing fine. We've had smaller ones than this. We can work near miracles here, Dan.'

'Twelve-week-early miracles?' he croaked, hating the intense warmth of the unit. That poor little mite. All those tubes…

'Oh, even earlier than that. Trust me.'

'I don't have any choice, do I?' he muttered.

And wanted to howl. Instead he gritted his teeth and went back to Helen to watch the video with her. When she cried her heart out at the sight of the tiny, helpless scraps of babies, he felt his chest fill to bursting.

The babies would be in an incubator, with machines monitoring their heart and lung function and temperature. They'd be fed intravenously and might need additional oxygen. If they even lived. It was all terrifying.

'It's very calm in the baby unit,' he said stiffly, trying to sound normal and positive. 'And you can visit any time. They take Polaroids—and we can take photos if we want and be with them as much as we like—'

'If they live,' she mumbled miserably, echoing his thoughts.

If she lived. The pain immobilised him. He wanted to give her a hug but kept his hands to himself and tried to be encouraging.

'It'll be OK, they've done this so many times,' he soothed.

'But I haven't! They haven't!' she sobbed.

'Helen!' He hesitated and tentatively stroked her shoulder, hopelessly impotent to do anything for her. Her plaintive face almost broke his control. But he had to be strong and reassuring. It was all he could do and he'd damn well stay calm for her sake. 'Sometimes,' he said gently, 'you have to put your faith in other people. You have to forget your fears and make a judgement based on what you know about them.'

Her tear-swilled eyes blinked up at him. 'Do you?' she snuffled.

'Of course. And we know all the best equipment is here, that the staff have the skills and experience, and that babies are able to survive even when they're very premature.'

'So...' She looked thoughtful. 'You're saying that we should trust someone if we know they've shown in the past that they can be relied on.'

'Sure.'

'It doesn't always work like that,' she said sadly.

'These are the experts. We have to put ourselves in their hands,' he insisted.

To his relief, she seemed calmed by what he'd said. The day wore on slowly, deadly hour followed by deadly hour. Dan fretted at the slowness of it all, hating the pain and anxiety that Helen was going through.

Then, in the early evening, she suddenly shouted in agony and clutched her abdomen just as the midwife popped in to check her.

'Dan! Stop it, stop the pain, I don't want it!' she yelled in despair.

'I wish I could,' he said fervently.

'Right. Labour ward for you,' said the nurse cheerfully, after a quick examination. 'Into the wheelchair. Come on, Daddy. Don't stand there rooted to the ground. This is it. Keep up.'

'Stay with me, Dan!' Helen cried frantically, her eyes huge with terror.

'Like glue!' he muttered grimly, catching her up.

His heart sounded like a steam hammer, bruising his chest. He was scared for her, afraid she'd die, but he couldn't let that show. Instead he helped her with the gas and air for the next few hours in the labour ward, and cheerily told her stories about work, about the plans he had for growing organic vegetables in the garden, where the children would go to school, everything, anything, to take her mind—and his—off the lurking fear of the unknown.

It got worse with every second that passed. Before this, he'd thought you had babies quickly. A lot of yelling and then there they were. Nobody ever showed this terrible, devastating waiting. It made him feel sick with apprehension, his guts and his bowels churning around in a terrible state.

And he'd never been frightened like this, not even when he'd been beaten up at school, because at least at that time he'd been able to do something, to fight back and kick and yell blue murder.

Here, he was helpless. A bystander. Totally useless.

'I wish I could have your pain,' he muttered to Helen.

'You're not the only one!' she panted heavily. 'Take it!' she yelled. 'Be—my—guest!'

'We're off,' announced the doctor suddenly after another check. 'You can come on up, Dan, but you must say goodbye outside Theatre. You can't come in,' he explained, 'because Helen's having an emergency Caesarean by general anaesthetic. Don't worry, you'll be a dad before you know it. OK, Mum?'

'No!' she wavered, remorselessly honest as always. 'Of course I'm not! I want to see my babies born!' she wailed.

'No can do. They're transverse—lying sideways instead of head or bottom down. Next time, maybe,' smiled the doctor.

'There won't be a flaming next time!' she shouted, making the nursing staff laugh indulgently.

It pained Dan that she was right. 'Here,' he said gruffly as they hurried her along the corridor. 'Hold my hand tightly and see if you can destroy each bone one by one.'

She gave a half-smile of gratitude. 'Silly.'

'Well, that's what you were doing earlier.'

'Was I? I'm sorry.'

'It wasn't much, compared with what you're going

through. Oh, and insist they stuff the babies back if they're not good-looking like us,' he whispered.

'Dan!' Helen giggled and then her face crumpled and she burst into tears.

'Oh, hell. Please don't cry...'

It was no good. He couldn't speak. There was so much he wanted to say but his throat was choked with tears and nothing was coming out. This was his opportunity to clear the air, to say how he felt.

Because there was a possibility that she might die.

He couldn't see. Damn it. Angrily he screwed a fist into his eye sockets and became aware that they were slowing down. This was it. And his mouth was giving way, refusing to hold its shape long enough to form words.

He bent and put his cheek against hers, holding her tightly, silently tasting her tears, hearing her choking sobs.

'I want you in there!' she whimpered. 'I don't want you to go! I feel safe with you!'

'I must go,' he said softly. 'I'll be outside. Ready to thump anyone who doesn't do their job right. OK?'

'Dan,' she sniffed. 'If—if anything hap-happens to me, you'll look after the babies, won't you?'

Oh, God. He couldn't handle that. All he could do was grunt and nod. Couldn't even assure her she'd come through this. Fat help he was.

But now he knew what she meant to him and what he was missing—would miss—by not being her husband in every sense. Whatever happened, he had lost the love of his life. And all because of Celine.

They were pulling him away, gently, kindly, but with firm insistence. He stood up, eyes swimming, and found a brave smile for her. Ruffled her hair. Patted her cheek. No words possible.

'See you soon, Dan,' she breathed, trying to be brave.

'We—we had good times together, didn't we?' she added plaintively.

He cracked up. Told her everything with his eyes, but by then she'd vanished into the operating theatre, a pathetic little face with enormous smoky eyes fixed on him. And he was left with a nurse patting his back soothingly.

Nothing had ever affected him so powerfully. If this was emotion then he wasn't sure he liked it.

He paced. Wished he smoked. Rang Diane, who was excited and concerned in equal measures. Spoke to Helen's parents again. Paced more furiously than ever, trying not to imagine what was going on inside there, what they were doing to Helen, to their tiny twins...

Ten minutes. He'd only been here ten lousy minutes! And he'd probably have an hour or more to wait and in that time he'd go mad...

He was walking miles up and down that corridor. Tried to work out how many, multiplying figures in his head to keep his mind off Helen's ordeal. It was a living nightmare and he wouldn't have wished it on anyone.

Sleepily, Helen opened her heavy eyelids, her mouth horribly dry.

'Helen!'

Smiling, she turned her head and saw Dan bending over her. 'Herro,' she mumbled stupidly.

'Thank God!'

'Mmm?'

'You're all right!'

'Woozy.' She blinked, remembering, and clutched Dan's arm. 'The babies! Are they...?'

'Fine,' he said, oddly husky.

She waited. He just stared down at her.

'Fine what? The variety, Dan! Boys, girls, budgies, werewolves—'

'Oh.' He grinned, sheepishly. 'A girl and a boy,' he said, as if savouring the words to himself.

'Wicked!' She smiled in delight. 'How lovely! One of each. That's clever of us. Details, Dan!' she urged. 'I missed it all, remember?'

'They were born at nine forty-one and nine forty-two,' he said softly, 'the girl first—'

'Typical. Impatient, like her mother,' she said happily. 'Weights?'

'Our son came in at three pounds, our daughter two ounces heavier. Quite a good weight, considering,' he said proudly.

'Our daughter. Our son,' she said with a dreamy sigh. 'Will they be all right? Really?'

'No reason why not.'

'Have you seen them?' she asked anxiously.

'Not yet. But I'm assured all the right bits are in the right places.' Dan cleared his throat. 'They'll take you up to the abour ward in a while, and make me up a bed next to you. You'll be monitored all the time. The babies, too. I can't believe that everything's OK. Staff here are wonderful, aren't they?'

'Mmm,' she agreed and promptly fell asleep.

Dan picked up the information books he'd been given about the prem unit and studied them carefully. All day he stayed with Helen, though she seemed spaced out most of the time. He didn't care. It meant he could stare at her, eat her up with his eyes, without her noticing. Over and over again he kept thinking how lucky they were, how blessed.

And then, at last, he was taken to see the twins. Their assigned nurse, Maggie, introduced herself and led him to the incubators. Stunned, he stared at the minute scraps of life, feeling a mixture of elation and deep shock at the same time. Being a father was incredible, but the babies were unnervingly small and the mass of wires and taped tubes seemed an insult to their tiny bodies.

Our babies. He couldn't take it in but knew his heart had already been claimed by them. It was lurching about all over the place.

'Can they really survive all this?' he asked quietly, sobered by the dangers to their tiny lives.

'It's early days, but there's no reason why they shouldn't. Their lungs haven't had time to develop properly, Dan, that's why they need help to breathe. They've been given caffeine as a stimulation and morphine for the shock of birth,' Maggie said gently. 'Your daughter is doing well and she may be off the oxygen soon.'

'And...my son?'

He swallowed, knocked sideways by the rush of emotion that had surged up when he'd said those words. My son. *My son. My daughter.* He said this to himself again and again, amazed at the thrill it gave him to be father to these babies: flesh of his flesh, bone of his bone. Part of him, part of Helen.

'He's not so strong, but that's the way with boys!' Maggie replied with a laugh. 'Get to know them, Dan. Talk to them. Sing, if you like.'

Choked up, he sat beside his daughter and fought for control as he studied the pathetic little body. She had eyelashes. And top-to-toe wrinkles. But she was beautiful in his eyes. A miracle.

'Hello, baby,' he said hoarsely. And began to whisper things; private, sentimental, loving. More than anything, he wanted these babies to be in his care. He ached to spend as much time as possible with them when they came out of hospital.

That meant one thing. He must see Celine as soon as he could get a spare hour or two. He would go to her when all this was over and the babies were home.

He stayed a while and then, suddenly needing human comfort, he went up to where Helen slept, stripped to his underwear and pulled his bed close so that he could put his arm around her. She stirred and smiled, snuggling closer.

And immediately his mind was filled with Celine. What he would do, what he'd say…hell, he could hardly wait.

He thought of how he'd walked out of the bathroom and seen her standing so boldly in that blue towel of Helen's and he couldn't stop himself from groaning. All his frustration would be solved once he'd seen her. It was a matter of patience. But he'd count the days, dear heaven, he'd count the minutes and seconds, too.

CHAPTER ELEVEN

AFTER three weeks, the twins—now lovingly named Kate and Mark—were transferred to Brighton and it was with mutual relief that Helen and Dan were able to return to live at Deep Dene. Since she couldn't drive for several weeks because of the Caesarean, he ferried her back and forth to the hospital and they spent all their waking time at the baby unit.

Helen's parents came, remaining—for the moment—blissfully unaware of the impending divorce. Helen felt she couldn't handle their distress. They adored Dan.

'Isn't he wonderful?' her mother marvelled, watching Dan singing to his son. 'No silly inhibitions about not being macho. Mind you, Dan could never look less than one hundred per cent masculine if he was wearing fluffy pink bedroom slippers, a tutu and an Alice band.'

Her father laughed and kissed his wife with affection. 'You're a lucky woman, Helen. You'll need his help and it looks as if he's more than willing to pull his weight. Look how he handles my grandson! And I swear little Mark turns to the sound of Dan's voice.'

'Yes,' she said shakily. 'He is amazing with them.'

'And you've settled well in your lovely home, and, judging by all the cards here, you've made lots of friends.'

'I have.'

The warmth of the villagers had been touching. They had taken her to their hearts with all their messages of goodwill. Dan, too, of course, though he'd been around less. But the shocked reaction of the people from the village would be another hurdle she'd have to face, when they learnt that she and Dan were to part.

Her mother sighed contentedly. 'We can go home knowing you're happy,' she said, giving Helen a fond kiss. 'You don't know how much that means to us, to see for ourselves that our daughter has no worries. Other than how to learn juggling so she can handle both babies at once,' she added with a grin.

'Oh, Mum!' she whispered, her eyes bright with tears. And she leaned over to grasp her mother's hand.

Her parents had been married for thirty-five years. She would have managed less than three.

Helen could feel her baby daughter's tiny little bottom nestling into the palm of her hand. And she knew that she wasn't giving Kate and Mark everything she wanted to.

Oh, with Dan's devotion they wouldn't lose out, but it wasn't what she'd visualised, it wasn't what she had planned for her children—parents who were polite and distant.

It shamed her that part of her was glad when her mother and father flew back to California. Keeping up the appearances of a normal relationship with Dan had been very difficult. He'd seemed determined to put his arm around her and kiss her more than was necessary, in an effort to convince her parents that nothing was wrong.

But she couldn't fault him where the babies were concerned. He was utterly devoted to them. It was he who, urged on by Maggie, first ventured to hold one in his big hands and even Maggie had wiped away a surreptitious tear to see the look on his face. Helen had just blubbed.

It was Dan, too, who had helped her to gain confidence in handling the babies until she'd become as capable as he was.

Sitting with Dan, she spent hours talking and singing and gently stroking the twins and they did seem to know their voices, as Maggie had promised they would, turning their funny little faces in the right direction. It was like winning the pools.

And with every day she adored them more, the bond between her and the twins strengthening till she realised what it truly was to give birth to children and to have your whole mind and body and emotions devoted to their welfare.

Each day they learnt something new about Kate and Mark. Gradually she and Dan became expert at interpreting the babies' body language: smooth and relaxed movements meaning they were fine, and tension or limpness meaning they weren't. Mark had been poorly for a while but was now putting on weight and Helen felt able to relax her vigilance at last, especially as the babies were in open incubators and could be properly cuddled.

She had to admit that Dan had been terrific. An absolute rock. In the early days in Portsmouth, apart from a quick shopping trip to get pyjamas and clean clothes and a couple of nighties for her, he hadn't left her side. Each night, especially when she'd been upset by little Mark's sudden poor health, he had fussed over her and been so attentive that she'd felt bemused and touched by his unselfishness.

He must have been worried, too, but he'd brushed aside her concern for him and concentrated on making sure she'd been reassured. A man in a million, she thought sadly, wishing he were *her* man in *her* million.

He'd had absolutely no time to himself and she worried about his loss of weight, his haggard looks and thin face, which only softened when he was with the babies.

His devotion was extraordinary and she knew she could trust him totally with the twins. As promised, he'd proved to be totally committed to them.

Why couldn't he give her the same amount of love and devotion? They were together all the time—and yet emotionally they were apart. With all her heart she wanted them to be reconciled.

'You look awful,' she commented to Dan, who was opening his shirt so that Kate—tubes and all—could be snuggled against his chest.

'Thanks,' he said drily. 'Come on, Kate. Snuggle up, sweetheart.'

With loving care, he closed his shirt around little Kate, giving her what Maggie called a 'kangaroo cuddle', and the baby visibly relaxed at the familiar skin-to-skin contact.

'You ought to take a break,' Helen said, engrossed in kangaroo cuddling herself. She looked down at her precious son who slept as if he hadn't a care in the world. Her heart ached with love for him. For them all. 'Dan, you must be worried about your business. You've been here all the hours of daylight and beyond. I won't think badly of you if you take time to catch up on work.'

'I couldn't!' he declared, shocked. 'It's not important, Helen. I learnt that when we went to Kirsty and Tom's. The important thing is that I—we—spend time with them now they need us. The business is doing well without me. I have someone I can trust at the helm. New contracts have come in and we're set for life.'

'But it's your...' She smiled wryly. 'It's your baby. You started it up. You made it what it was. Don't you miss it?'

'I haven't given it a thought, to be honest. My work is not as important as this. You need a chauffeur and you also need another pair of hands. That's my role for the time being.'

Helen kissed the top of Mark's small head. He was right. He needed time to bond with the children. She watched him shaking a rattle gently, in an attempt to gain Kate's attention.

'Hello, Kate!' he cooed. 'Look at Daddy!'

She couldn't bear it and took a deep breath, her nerves frayed. She remembered what he'd said about putting your trust in someone if they had a track record of reliability.

She thought of Dan's devotion to the babies, his tenderness and the huge well of love that he was offering to his children. And wanted part of that love.

His behaviour had opened her eyes again. They'd had a falling-out and now it was time to heal the breach before it was too late.

Nervously she gathered up all her courage and went for it.

'I—I'd rather you had another role,' she said huskily. Her smoke-dark eyes met his startled gaze. Tenderly she stroked Mark's cheek, her eyes soft with passion. 'We have so much in common. All those years we spent together... Couldn't we...? Oh, Dan, if you only said you were sorry for betraying me with Celine, I—'

'I can't,' he said tersely, his face grim.

Helen stared in dismay. He was lifting Kate out, putting her back in the heated cot. Doing up his shirt. She felt a terrible hollow sensation in the pit of her stomach.

'Why not?' she breathed. 'If a simple apology would mean that we could be together properly—'

'No, Helen!'

Dear heaven, she thought. He looks terrible. Angry and wounded.

'I want you back!' she mumbled plaintively.

His jaw quivered. 'Then you must trust me totally. Believe in me.'

The wobbling of her mouth almost stopped her from answering.

'No woman on earth would witness that scene with Celine and believe what you said!' she declared miserably.

Dan eyed her with such sadness that she felt her heart would break.

'I'll have the car outside in two hours,' he said in a remote tone. And walked out.

Helen spent the time in deep thought. Finally she came to the conclusion that her wounded pride was getting in the way. She and Dan could make a go of their marriage, she knew it. That meant…that she must trust him.

It was as if a weight had been lifted from her shoulders. They'd start again, wiser, more loving than before.

All through the drive home, she kept smiling secretly to herself, knowing what she'd do. Dan disappeared into his study as usual, and she went straight upstairs to put on something that flattered her slowly returning figure and then headed for the woodshed.

Axe in hand, she sauntered into the hall and lifted the axe with great care not to strain her 'nice little bikini cut'—though by now she felt as fit as a fiddle. And brought the blade crashing down against the door of Dan's flat.

There was a yell from inside and she quickly dealt it another blow.

'Helen!' he bellowed. 'Stop! You'll hurt yourself!'

She waited and the door was cautiously opened. Her huge eyes regarded him solemnly.

'If you feel like that about me,' he said jerkily, 'then get someone else to beat me up. Don't hurt yourself, please, Helen.'

Delighted that he was thinking of her, she smiled and lowered the axe. 'I was only breaking the door down,' she said, all innocence.

'I'd gathered that,' he said with a grunt.

'Ask me why.'

He gave an exasperated sigh and humoured her. 'Why?'

'Because I don't want you to live in a flat. I don't want you and me to be living separately when the twins come home. I want us to be properly together; married, normal, parents.'

'We've tried that—'

'Listen to me, Dan,' she said softly, coming closer. He gave his collar a very satisfyingly nervous tweak. 'I've watched you with Kate and Mark. I could trust you with them totally. And I reckon that you wouldn't do anything that might jeopardise their future.'

'No. Of course I wouldn't—'

'So I feel that I can trust you, too. I don't care about Celine any more. It doesn't matter to me either way what happened. You are everything I've always wanted and I don't intend to let you become estranged from me any longer. Come back to me, Dan. No questions, no recriminations, just you and me and our children. I love you. I've always loved you. I want you to trust me.'

'You believe me?'

'I trust you.'

Starved of affection, she walked straight into his waiting arms. He gave a huge sigh and kissed her. Hard. They went into the sitting room and sat together, just content to be in one another's embrace.

Now she was happy. Her heart was full. And that night they curled up body to body, sleeping more deeply than either of them had done so for weeks.

Christmas was wonderful. New Year, too. Helen had never known such happiness could exist. By the time the twins were three months old—and their 'proper' birth date of late January was reached—they had gained sufficient weight to be released from hospital. They were coming home and all the worries, all the tiring journeys to and from the hospital were over.

'I'm stopping for supplies. Will you be OK for a while, or do you want to come round the supermarket with me?'

Dan asked on the way back, their precious cargo safely secured in two navy and white striped car seats.

Helen turned her head and took her thousandth smug glance at the sleeping babies. They were adorable. Kate had Dan's thick black hair and Mark boasted Dan's fabulous black lashes. Their little faces had filled out and Dan claimed that Kate was going to have her mother's classically beautiful features and long legs. They were the most beautiful babies she'd ever seen. Of course. She smiled blissfully and turned back to Dan.

'We did the shopping yesterday. That's enough, surely? Can't we go straight home?' she asked wistfully.

'I'd love to. But I'm worried about the level of the river,' Dan replied. 'It's rained so much over this year that the ground is saturated and there are severe flood warnings on our river. The last thing we want is to be stranded and run out of nappies. I'd like to get in an extra store of food, in case there's trouble. Just as a precaution.'

'You're right. We'll be fine in the car. I'll listen to the radio. You'll be able to scoot around faster without us in tow. We'd be sure to draw a crowd!'

Dan laughed and squeezed Helen's hand. 'I know! I think we'll have to build in cooing time for any trips out. And I suppose we ought to be careful about crowds. The babies still need protection. They're very tiny still.'

'I love you, Dan,' she said softly, stroking his arm. And melted at his warm answering smile.

He'd been right about the flood levels. All around Lewes the fields had been turned into lakes. The radio had forecast more storms and put out warnings to people in flood plains. When they set off again from the supermarket, the rain began to lash the car and she felt glad of Dan's foresight in stocking up.

A while later she was frowning at the sight of the lane

ahead into the village, which had water rushing across it from a higher field to a lower.

'It wasn't like this when we left early this morning,' she worried. 'Oh, Dan! Can we make it?'

'Of course,' he soothed. 'It's not too deep.'

'What if we're at home and we're cut off and the twins are ill?' she asked, holding her breath as the four-wheel drive approached the churning water.

'If I thought we were risking their health,' Dan replied, carefully negotiating the flood, 'I'd turn right back and check into a hotel in Brighton, near the hospital. But remember, the doctor is on the same ridge as us and we can reach him across the top fields if necessary.'

'Is he?'

'He and I were patting ourselves on the back for vowing never to live below the hundred-foot contour line. There. We're through. OK?'

'You're wonderful, Dan!' she declared in relief. 'We're so lucky to have you.'

'That's true,' he acknowledged, and received a light punch in the arm for his pains. 'Mobile's ringing, bully. Can you answer it?'

'Everything all right?' came the doctor's voice.

'Wonderful!' she sighed.

'Nearly home, I hope?' he enquired.

'Five minutes to go—' She frowned. The phone had gone dead. 'It was Dr Taylor, seeing if we were OK,' she informed Dan. 'I think he must have been called away.'

'Good of him to ring. He's been great.'

'I'm so excited!' she cried as they neared their house. There was the rutted lane, the hedge, the high flint wall...and Deep Dene. 'Good grief!' she exclaimed. 'What's going on?' Her eyes twinkled and she grinned. 'Oh, Dan! It's a welcoming party! Look at the banner!'

Welcome home, Kate and Mark. Her eyes blurred with

tears. Home. Where she and Dan and the babies would carve a safe and secure future. Where they would be happy, loved and loving. Where Dan could at last know the joys of a caring, tender family.

'Don't cry, sweetheart,' Dan said fondly, passing her his handkerchief. 'They'll think I've been shouting at you. Look. There must be about fifteen people there. Have you *that* many friends who are prepared to stand in the rain for you?' he asked in amusement.

'I s-suppose s-so,' she sniffed, waving madly at everyone. They hoisted aloft their colourful umbrellas and raised a soggy cheer. 'Poor things! We must get them all inside! They'll catch their deaths standing in the rain like this!' she exclaimed in horror. 'How long have they been waiting, for heaven's sake?'

'Well, the doc rang to see where we were, remember? So I imagine they timed it from then. Still, it's incredibly kind of them to turn out on such a foul day. Here we are. Bale out. I'll see to the babies, you get inside and put the kettle on.'

Helen found herself beneath the shelter of several umbrellas, carried forwards on a wave of love and smiling faces. Turning back as she opened the front door, she saw willing hands helping Dan with the twins and beginning to unload the huge store of groceries.

'Welcome home,' enthused Dr Taylor, hugging her. 'You look absolutely radiant.'

And she was lost in hugs, whirled from one to another until she ended up locked in Dan's arms.

'Hello, darling,' he said, a rapturous smile lighting his eyes with love. And, oblivious to the crowd around them, he kissed her tenderly, to a chorus of 'ah-h-h's.'

Blushing, Helen organised the hanging-up of wet coats and the shedding of boots. The twins slept on, oblivious to the careful peeks and admiring sighs.

'I'm bursting with happiness,' she said to Dan, helping him to open bottles of champagne.

'Not over my clean floor, you won't,' he warned.

She giggled. He'd spent ages cleaning the house for her while she'd lain like Lady Muck on the sofa, sipping tea and toast before they'd gone off to collect the babies.

'I'm going to whip Kate and Mark away,' she said. 'Time they had their feed. And I think that's enough strangers breathing over them for the time being. I'll go upstairs. See you later.'

She said her thanks and farewells, knowing it would take her ages to feed the babies. Overwhelmed by the unexpected affection, she was sniffing happily by the time she'd said goodbye to everyone, the tears pouring down her cheeks.

'I'll take Kate up,' Dan offered. 'You bring Mark. Our guests will be OK with the champagne and nibbles for a moment.' In the bedroom he settled her comfortably and shrugged off his jacket in the cosy warmth of the house. 'I'll pop down for a moment. See you in a while. Love you, darling,' he said huskily.

He kissed her. Kissed the top of Kate's head and watched his daughter suckling for a moment, for all the world as if she was the most incredible and perfect baby in the world. Which she was, equally with Mark, of course, Helen thought with a contented sigh.

Dan tiptoed out. God, she was happy.

'My darling babies,' she whispered, looking over at dark-haired, gorgeous little Mark, who was only just waking and beginning to utter tiny protests of hunger. He had the sweetest face. The bluest of eyes. Her heart fluttered with unbounded love.

Dan's mobile beeped. Realising it must be in his jacket pocket, she used her free hand to slip it out, discovering that the mobile must be in text mode. Without thinking, she accessed it.

She stiffened as the message appeared on the screen.

'Hi. Celine,' it said.

Helen froze. That woman! How dared she? The message scrolled on.

'Can't make Friday. Change to Thursday?'

Helen's eyes widened in horror. Frantically she clutched Kate to her, reading the betraying text.

'Things so good 4 us,? step up meetings? 3 x week not 2? Next weeks are precious. Yes?! Let me know. So happy. Will deal with Helen 2day. Love C.'

CHAPTER TWELVE

So MUCH for fidelity, Helen thought, feeling a pain slicing her in two. Betrayed. Again.

She wanted to scream and howl and tear the bed sheets to pieces in her rage and despair. But she had to stay calm and finish feeding the babies. They came before everything. Even grief.

Noise in the hall below told her that people were going and she heard their good wishes ringing out, the laughter, the cheery affection that always came with the arrival of little babies.

On a sudden impulse, she reached out and deleted the message on the phone, not knowing what she'd do, only that her whole life was being re-drawn.

Dan came up some time later when she was changing Mark. 'You look tired, darling,' he said gently. 'Shall I take over?'

She nodded. 'Headache,' she mumbled, not looking at him.

His hand stroked her forehead. Massaged the back of her neck and shoulders. Hypocrite! she thought.

'They're sleeping now. You have a lie down. I'll wake you for tea.'

Limp and malleable in her misery, she let him tuck her under the counterpane, her throbbing head sinking into the pillow with relief.

Sleep evaded her. She stared up at the ceiling blankly, quite paralysed by his deceit. He wanted it all. Wife, children, mistress. A stable home, fun and frolics with fringed knickers. Perhaps that was what all men wanted.

But of course she would never agree to such a cosy, convenient arrangement. Dan must leave. He was asking too much of her.

She heard his feet then, running up the stairs. Alerted by his urgency, she sat up in alarm.

'What is it? What are you doing?' she demanded in panic when he ignored her, hurrying straight to the wardrobe and flinging the doors open.

'Call from the doc. The river's burst its bank,' he said tersely, grabbing an old pair of thick jeans and a cable-knit sweater. 'Combination of high tide and floods upstream.'

He saw his mobile on the table and picked it up then yanked off his clothes and hauled on the jeans while Helen stared, confused.

'Are we in danger?' she asked anxiously. 'You said we were safe—'

'We are.' Yanking the jumper on at a run, he paused in the doorway. 'It's the other poor devils in the village who are in trouble. Water's six feet deep. You must cope alone for a while, Helen. I'm going out to bring people back here.'

She leapt out of bed, running down the stairs with him, her heart thudding frantically. 'Dan! You could get into serious danger—!'

'So could they,' he said grimly. 'Be prepared with towels and hot soup or something. Leave it to you.' He kissed her hard on the mouth. 'Bye,' he said huskily, pulling on his waterproofs and jamming his feet into boots. 'Take care.'

Opening the door, they saw how far the water had come. The lane was awash. Fields beyond were unrecognisable. The flooding was severe, the rain non-stop stair-rods. And Dan was going out in this.

'Dan!' she wailed, frightened for him.

'Go inside. I'll be fine!' he yelled, halfway to the car. 'See you soon.'

And he was gone.

Helen didn't stop to think. She plugged in the baby alarm and grabbed towels from the airing cupboard, then hurtled down the stairs to make preparations.

He must live, she thought to herself. Even if it was so that he could go off to Celine. It didn't matter, only that he was safe.

For almost an hour she stood by the window, watching for any sign of him. And then, to her relief, she saw lights through the lashing rain and the wonderful sight of his car turning into the drive.

Helen rushed to flick on the kettle and hurried to welcome the first flood survivors. Over the next few hours, Dan ferried in several cold, wet and shivering groups of people—some of whom were the same friends who had made up their welcome home party.

Although she was busy looking after everyone and dispensing tea, warm soup and cheerful *bonhomie*, she constantly feared for Dan's life. It was dark now. If she stood by the open door she could hear the water roaring down the lane.

A kind hand caught hers and she turned her terrified gaze to see the sympathetic face of Mrs Reid, from the village post office. 'He'll be all right,' she said gently. 'He won't take any unnecessary risks, not with you and the babies here.'

'Won't he?' she mumbled, thinking that no one here knew Dan at all. They'd be shocked if she yelled out he was a liar and a cheat. An adulterer without a conscience, smiling, pretending to be in love...

'Come on, love,' soothed Mrs Reid. 'You look all in. Take a break and we can all manage now we know where everything is.'

'There's beds to organise—' she began shakily.

'And babies to mother. You see to them when they need you, and see to your man when he comes home. We can get blankets and cushions and set up camp in the sitting room. And we can peel some spuds for chips. Sit down, have a cup of tea and keep your strength for where it's needed.'

She was forced into a chair. Her man. Huh. She had no claim on him. He only wanted the babies and, because she came with them, he had to let her tag along, too.

It grew very late. Many of the dozen people Dan had brought back were snoozing or talking quietly in the kitchen by the roaring fire in the inglenook. Cold and de-spairing, she fed the twins again and settled them for their night-time sleep.

Then she stood by the hall window, watching, waiting, a terrible sucking sensation in her stomach as the time dragged by and there was no sign of Dan.

When the phone rang, she leapt for it in one bound. 'Yes?' she answered in a panicky voice.

'Me. I'll be back in ten minutes. Just checking with the doc that between us we've got everyone to safety. Are you all right, darling?'

'Yes,' she said tinnily. 'Oh, thank heaven you're alive! I was so scared! Come back. Come back soon. Take care—'

'Of course I will. I wouldn't risk our happiness now for anything.'

She sniffed, beguiled by the silken words. 'Wouldn't you?'

'Never, my darling. Never in a million years.'

His warm, golden voice washed over her. There must be some mistake, she thought suddenly. Or perhaps Celine was up to her tricks again. This was a test of her belief in him. Could she risk her heart and trust him?

'Please come back safely,' she whispered.

'You bet. Save me a cuddle. Can we cope with one more family? The doctor is stacking them up two deep and we can manage, can't we? Seven people. A young mother, her five children—one is a two-month-old baby— and the grandfather. The doc's checked them over. The old man's shaking like a leaf and the mother's petrified for her kiddies—'

'Bring them,' she said firmly. 'We have plenty of willing hands here.'

She took the mother and children under her wing when they arrived, barely taking time to do more than hug Dan briefly. Later, when mother and the youngest children were all tucked up in her big bed, the older ones curled up on plump duvets on the floor, Helen watched Dan relaxing the old man with reminiscences about the village in the past.

'Deserves a medal,' said a sleepy Mrs Reid, looking up at Helen.

She nodded, her expression solemn. 'A good man. Kind. Thoughtful.'

'Keep hold of him, love. Don't let him go.'

'No,' said Helen slowly. 'I won't.'

And she walked over to Dan, kissing him on the forehead and looping an arm around his shoulders, joining in the amiable chat with the old man. She and Dan would work things out. All these people had put their trust in him. So could she.

'Where are we sleeping, darling?' he asked when they'd settled the old man.

He rubbed a weary hand over his five o'clock shadow and she felt her heart lurch. He'd put himself through hell to give virtual strangers a warm, dry bed for the night— and perhaps for the foreseeable future.

'With the babies. Two of the men put their little cots in

the boxroom for me. It's a single bed so we'll have to breathe in all night.'

'Come on. Everyone else is asleep now. Let's get what sleep we can. We've one hell of a breakfast to organise in the morning!'

Helen laughed and held his hand as they went up the stairs. 'I think there'll be plenty of cooks.'

She glanced in on their bedroom and the sleeping children. The young mother was nestled up in the big bed with two kiddies, the baby tucked up in a drawer, quite peaceful and unaware of the drama. She and Dan smiled at one another.

'I love you,' he said softly.

'I know.' And she did. Had never felt so sure.

'I'd make love to you but I'm bushed. Cuddle?'

'Please.'

Gently she helped him out of his clothes and held him close, her eyes bright with tears as she breathed into his shoulder.

'Was it dangerous?' she asked.

His lips found her temple. 'Yes. I have to admit, it was. The current was so strong that I had to fight to keep the car on the lane—not that I could see where the lane was. But someone was watching over me. And I was sure I'd be OK. I knew I couldn't have found happiness only for it to be torn from my grasp.' He laughed, drawing her down to the bed and helping her to undress. 'I had a phone call halfway through one dodgy manoeuvre. I was lifting the old man out of a window when my mobile rang. I thought it was you and hurriedly helped the poor guy into the car so I could see what was the matter. It turned out to be Celine! I could have brained her! But she wasn't to know what I was doing of course.'

Helen's heart missed a beat. 'Oh?' She tried to sound casual. 'What did she want?'

'To step up our meetings. And if you're wondering why I'd meet her, well…I can tell you now,' he murmured, kissing the nape of her neck and holding her tightly. 'She's my PA. Are you annoyed?'

'Should I be?' she breathed tensely.

'Lie down,' he coaxed, snuggling up to her. His mouth wandered over her jaw. 'After what happened before, you might. When I knew you were expecting twins,' he went on quietly, 'I realised that I had to quickly find someone who could take over and run the business end efficiently. Diane had said there was only one person who could do that without hours and hours of training. So I bit the bullet, rang Celine and offered her a substantial rise in salary.'

And what more did he offer? she wondered, with a brief flash of her old doubts.

'She took a lot of persuading. We'd had a spectacular row after that time she pranced about in your blue towel. Because I'd been shocked by her behaviour I said some pretty hard things to her. But we talked things through and she came round, eventually.'

Persuaded how? Helen thought.

'She's been brilliant, sweetheart,' he crooned. 'She's brought in some highly lucrative contracts. My hunch worked. I'm making her a partner.'

Helen closed her eyes. The woman would always be there. A spectre. A ghoul, haunting her, denying the total happiness she'd imagined…

'You must know that I love you,' Dan said softly. 'You are everything to me. I fell in love with you the moment I saw you in your pigtails and school uniform, chatting to Ted Downey by the bike shed. I adore your kind heart, your funny turns of phrase, your optimism and joy and wild exaggerations. I love every part of you to pieces.' His voice shook. 'I have never, ever, been unfaithful to you, not even in thought. I couldn't be. You absorb my whole mind and body and soul. Every part of me is tuned to you and you alone. And I will feel like that till the day I die.'

There had been a solid truth in every word. Helen tried to think beyond the events that had made her doubt him and concentrated on Dan himself. Her furrowed brow cleared.

'I know that,' she said huskily. And he held her so tightly that she could hardly breathe.

'I knew when I married you that it would be for ever. When you saw Celine and me, half naked, apparently caught red-handed in some love-tryst, I was appalled.' He gave a rueful laugh. 'My jaw must have dropped to the floor.'

'I thought you were struck dumb by her beautiful body.'

Dan looked shocked. 'By disbelief,' he corrected. 'I couldn't believe what she was doing. It was like a bad dream. I'll never forget that moment as long as I live.' He shuddered. 'And your reaction was unnerving. I could hardly speak for fear and anger.'

'Anger with me?' she asked.

'Yes. I was angry with her, too. I know we must have looked guilty but I was shaken rigid that you thought I could ever have cheated on you, and lied to you as well. Her stupid little game had put our marriage in jeopardy. All I could do was to hope you'd know that I would never throw away what we had between us. But Celine threw a spanner in the works by pretending we'd been lovers.'

'But you hadn't, had you?' she said, her confidence growing.

'No, darling. I love you so much!' he said passionately. His black eyes blazed in the darkness. 'And later I made it worse by ringing her. I wanted her to tell you the truth—'

'And I heard, and thought you were making an assignation.' Her hand stroked his face. 'Poor Dan. You must have been frantic.'

'I was. I would have called her again immediately after that but you'd fainted and my mind was pre-occupied with the fact that you were pregnant. I kept trying to reach her but she'd changed her mobile number. Eventually Diane let me know how to contact her—Celine had asked for a reference—and that's when I managed to take her on the payroll again. But she wouldn't talk to you because she was too ashamed of what she'd done. So I knew that my only hope was to make you realise that I could be relied on.'

'You never said anything when I said I'd cite Celine in our divorce,' she reminded him softly.

'I couldn't say anything, full-stop. My emotions got the better of me. I was close to breaking down totally.'

'Oh, my poor darling. I love you. I believe you,' she whispered.

Dan drew back a little, his face radiant. 'So...you'd come to Celine's wedding?' he asked with a twinkle in his eyes.

'Her...what?'

'She's fallen madly in love with one of my clients,' he explained with a chuckle. 'And finally she's plucked up courage to talk to you because she wants no bad feeling. She tried to get hold of me earlier and thought she'd left a message but something must have gone wrong with the connection. But you see, time is of the essence for her. She needs us to get everything that's outstanding in the business safely under wraps before she goes on honeymoon.'

Helen smiled, remembering the text message. 'I see,' she murmured.

'In fact Celine was so anxious about seeing you that she decided to come over today. The doc picked her up in the village earlier, from her stranded car. She's one of his flood refugees.' He kissed Helen gently on the lips, his mouth lingering a while, his eyes dancing in amusement. 'I thought it unwise to bring her here till I'd primed you.'

Snuggling into his warm body, Helen laughed softly. 'In case I tore her hair out?'

He grinned. 'You were terrifying.'

The breath caught in her throat. The movement of his hand over her body was electrifying. But he was tired.

'Sleep,' she soothed.

'To hell with sleep,' he growled.

Her mouth went dry. 'Dan!' she whispered in delight.

'I want you,' he muttered passionately. 'Want you, need you, adore you, hunger every moment of my life for you. Love me, Helen.'

His mouth claimed hers in total possession and her body leapt with joy. The harsh abrasion of his unshaven chin rasped over her shoulder as his kisses wandered in frantic, moaning fervour.

She thought she would die of love, falling, falling deeply, helplessly into a whirling pool of magical sensation where the touch of Dan's body was the focus of her whole mind, her heart, her very soul.

He loves me, she thought ecstatically. Loves me.

Sliding against him, kissing, nibbling, demanding, she let her heart flow to his. Delicate, agonisingly erotic flames began to ignite every part of her and she was trying to suppress her moans, releasing her need to yell by sheer physical action.

Winding her legs around him. Flinging her head back, lifting her heavy breasts for him, enticing his fingers lower and lower, her eyes luring him on, mouth soft and supple as it aroused his lips, his hard, sensitive nipples and the wonderful manliness of him.

The heat of him within her made her almost cry with

pleasure. The firmness of his mouth on hers told her what it meant to him, too. This was the beginning of their life together as a real family. The promise of love and joy to come.

Of trust and support. A lifetime of loving.

'I love you!' he said roughly. 'More than you could ever know.'

'My darling,' she whispered, her eyes glistening with happy tears. 'I know. Oh, I do know.'

Within her, the silk of him slid in the first movements of its pagan rhythm. Helen closed her eyes and gave herself to it. And to Dan.

His hands gripped her shoulders tightly and she lifted her lashes to watch as his climax neared. He was beautiful. The dark crescents of his lashes fluttered in a delicious agony, his lips parted as he whispered her name over and over again.

And she knew no more, only the wonderful escape of her body and her mind to that total surrender of herself, the moment when they were indivisible.

'Sweetheart, sweetheart,' he groaned.

'Dan!'

Their bodies meshed, limbs damp with sweat, muscles taut as they reached the peak of sensation and began to sink into the warm comfort of the aftermath.

'So much for tiredness,' she mumbled sleepily.

'You'd arouse a brick wall,' he growled.

'I do the jokes.'

'Forgot.'

She gave a beatific smile and nestled in his arms. They had faced the edge of the precipice in their marriage and had survived. And now she could relax and enjoy life to the full.

Although the villagers were worried about their houses, they were remarkably cheerful in the morning, happily munching cereal and toast and bacon and egg cooked—as Helen had predicted—by a group of amiable helpers.

For two days the water level remained at danger level. The adults invented hilarious games to keep the children amused and Helen and Dan were swamped with offers to help with the twins who gurgled and chuckled happily at everyone who came to admire and entertain them.

Beside blazing fires, the villagers chatted and whiled away the long, dark evenings, and Helen adored watching Dan: the firelight glowing on his handsome face and high-lighting its planes and hollows, his happiness so transparent that everyone who looked at him was forced to smile in response.

This was his extended family, she thought as they cuddled their beautiful babies and talked softly with everyone into the night. The babies they might so nearly have lost. The husband she might never have had.

This was what Dan and she had always longed for. The house might look like a refugee camp with beds and clothes strewn about and bodies and bustle and chaos everywhere, but it was filled with laughter and fun and the closeness that came with shared troubles. She and Dan were a special part of the village now. Family.

Eventually the water went down sufficiently for some of them to assess the damage to their homes. Dan went, too, to lend a hand with shifting furniture or lifting sodden carpets. Those who stayed at Deep Dene kept telling Helen how much they admired Dan. And she agreed fervently.

During Dan's absence, Helen found herself facing a frightened looking Celine when she opened the front door. To Helen's surprise she was in a very severe tailored suit and no sign of killer heels or sassy pink anywhere, just a plain white shirt and sensible mid-height court shoes.

But Helen was far too happy to feel angry. Her smile

took Celine aback and the woman burst into floods of tears.

'Quickly. Come into Dan's study,' Helen said sympathetically, her arm around Celine's shaking shoulders. 'It's the only place I can guarantee privacy.'

'Oh, Helen! I'm so sorry,' Celine said wretchedly. 'Can I explain?' she asked.

'Of course. Sit down.'

Celine did so, very upright, very proper. She placed a carrier bag on the floor beside her, took a deep breath and began to talk very fast, her face white and frightened.

'I'll start at the beginning. I made a fool of myself, basically,' Celine confessed. 'You see, Dan had been talking about you a lot in the office, about how he was worried you weren't happy with the house and how you two hardly saw one another. He was working frantically hard so he could buy you a flat in London as a surprise—'

'A *what*?' exclaimed Helen. 'They cost the *earth*!'

'I know. But he didn't care. He thought it might be the solution. He was terrified some guy at work would grab you and take you away from him.' Embarrassed, Celine looked down at her neatly manicured hands—no coloured polish, Helen noticed. 'Oh, I could sink into the ground with shame, Helen, for what I did! He's fantastic, is Dan. And I felt sorry for him and thought I was in love with him. I got it into my head that you weren't appreciating him and that he'd fall for me if I could only get him into bed. I'm so ashamed. He'd done nothing to encourage me. Honestly. I hadn't realised how crazy he was about you, and that he'd be screaming blue murder because I'd destroyed his marriage. I hid his clothes....' She picked up the bag and handed it to Helen shame-facedly.

Helen looked inside and drew a breath. The missing suit and shirt, complete with coffee stains. She looked up, her eyes querying this.

'I shoved it behind a chest in the hall before I—before I took all my clothes off,' Celine muttered, blushing to the roots of her hair.

'And you then arranged your clothes on the stairs?' Helen asked gently.

Celine nodded, her face a picture of misery. 'I can hardly bear to think of it! When—when I eventually left in the taxi, I took his clothes home and stowed them away in the back of my wardrobe—then promptly forgot them. Dan came round and tore strips off me that left me raw and bleeding inside. I realised then how badly I'd behaved. It was a cheap and wicked thing to do. I know that now, and I badly want your forgiveness, Helen. I want to start afresh and get this off my back. It's hanging over me like the sword of Damocles and I want everything sorted before my marriage so that I feel clean and decent again. Please forgive me.'

Helen went over and sat beside the shaking Celine. 'Of course I do,' she said softly. 'How can I blame you for adoring the man I think is the most wonderful person in the world?' She smiled and hugged Celine who burst into tears of relief. 'I almost ought to be annoyed with you for falling in love with someone else!' she said with a teasing laugh.

Celine brightened up. 'Oh, Helen, John is just perfect! I've never known anyone so kind and gentle and understanding. He's made me feel so much better about myself. I've found happiness that I never knew could exist. Real happiness. Based on love.'

Helen blinked. Those weren't the qualities she would have thought mattered to Celine. What a funny old world.

'Tell me about him,' she urged.

A bliss that Helen recognised as besotted love infused Celine's face. 'I was arranging for Dan to organise the

records for a church charity and John was my contact.
He's the canon at my local church—'

Helen blinked. 'A man of the cloth?'

'I know! I can hardly believe it myself!' laughed Celine.
'But now I know what a truly good man is like. Dan is
that, too, of course. Perhaps that's why I thought I was in
love with him. I've been hurt so much, Helen. I've always
chosen rotters before and—well, they put sex on the top
of their agenda, with caring and consideration nowhere to
be seen. I've come to my senses. John, well, he's been
married and widowed and is much older than me, but he
adores me and thinks I'm wonderful even though I don't
deserve him...'

Helen listened attentively while Celine described her fi-
ancé in detail. 'He sounds perfect for you,' she said
warmly, her hand closing over Celine's.

'Dan said you were fantastic,' Celine declared. 'And
he's right. Thank you for listening, for not showing me
the door. It's meant a lot to me.' She smiled. 'I'd better
be going. Get out of your way—'

'No. Stay. Let him see that there's no ill feeling between
us,' Helen suggested.

The two women hugged and Helen led the tearful Celine
back into the kitchen. Dan had returned. He was sitting on
the sofa with both babies in his arms, an adoring public
eagerly listening to his reports on the floods.

Every time he looked down at the twins his face became
suffused with adoration. Their tiny hands had captured his
fingers, gripping tightly and making him a willing pris-
oner.

Helen felt a huge whoosh of emotion flood through her
as she watched the tableau: her beloved babies, her darling
husband.

Dan saw her, smiled at Celine and offered Helen a more
bone-melting smile, his tar-black eyes melting in an in-

vitation she couldn't resist. Slipping into the space beside him and taking Kate in her arms, she snuggled up in the circle of Dan's arm.

Home with my loved ones, she thought. How wonderful.

'Everything all right, darling?' he asked softly.

'Perfect,' she husked.

And didn't care when his tender kiss brought a chorus of 'ooh!'s from the laughing neighbours all around them. She was deeply proud of her brave and loyally steadfast husband. And she didn't care who knew it.

'Don't cry, darling.'

Dan dabbed at Helen's eyes tenderly with his handkerchief.

'It's...they're so little—'

'They're almost five, sweetheart. And look how excited they are to be at school!' he soothed.

'I know.' She got a hold of her emotions and watched Kate and Mark playing with their friends in the village school field, just before the start of the autumn term. 'I'm being silly. I'll miss them so much.'

'They break you in gently,' Dan said in amusement. 'Mornings only for a while. So kind of them to think of the parents, isn't it?'

She laughed. 'Idiot!'

Fondly they stood with the other parents who were leaning over the fence, watching their children enjoying the warm September sunshine. Because the village was a close-knit community, everyone knew everyone else, and Helen knew that the twins wouldn't find it hard to settle.

Kate was tall for her age; delicate-boned and foal-like, with long dark hair and a lively manner. The village ballet class had already captured Kate's heart and the little girl was beautiful and graceful to watch as she practised in the hall at home.

Mark had Dan's strength and dependability. With his dark, wavy hair, he now had coal-black eyes and a ready smile, and women of all ages found themselves smiling at him. But she knew he wouldn't be a heartbreaker. Mark was too like his father for that. He'd treat women with kindness and courtesy, adoring them but never hurting them.

'I love them so much,' Helen said softly.

'Me, too. And I adore you.' Dan kissed her. 'So, Mrs Shaw,' he murmured, his eyes pooling deliciously, 'we have the morning to ourselves. Any ideas how we might fill it?'

'I have a load of washing and you must surely have work to do,' she said, with a look of mock innocence.

'Washing. Hmm.' He looked her up and down. 'I think we could both do with a long, sensual bath.'

Helen ignored the fact that they'd both had a shower that morning. 'With drawn curtains and candles. Chocolates. Music—'

'Bye, Kate!' Dan yelled. 'Bye, Mark!'

The twins whirled around, their little faces bright with happiness. They both hurtled to the fence and Dan and Helen leaned over for their kisses.

'Have a lovely time,' she said to them both.

'We will!' they cried in glee and shot off.

'And so will we,' Dan murmured. 'Trust me.'

'Implicitly,' she whispered. 'Implicitly.'

FALL IN LOVE
THIS WINTER
WITH
HARLEQUIN BOOKS!

In October 2002 look for these special volumes
led by *USA TODAY* bestselling authors,
and receive a MOULIN ROUGE VHS video*!
*Retail value of $14.99 U.S.

See inside books for details.

***This exciting promotion
is available at your
favorite retail outlet.***

Only from

HARLEQUIN®
Makes any time special ®

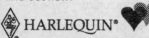

**Lindsay Armstrong...
Helen Bianchin...
Emma Darcy...
Miranda Lee...**

Some of our bestselling writers are Australians!

Look our for their novels about the Wonder from Down Under—where spirited women win the hearts of Australia's most eligible men.

THE AUSTRALIANS

Coming soon:

THE MARRIAGE RISK
by Emma Darcy
On sale February 2001, Harlequin Presents® #2157

And look out for:

MARRIAGE AT A PRICE
by Miranda Lee
On sale June 2001, Harlequin Presents® #2181

Available wherever Harlequin books are sold.

HARLEQUIN®
Makes any time special ™

Visit us at www.eHarlequin.com   HPAUS